RITUAL SLAUGHTER

NEW CANADIAN NOVELISTS SERIES

The *New Canadian Novelists Series* from Quarry Press
charts new directions being taken in contemporary Canadian
fiction by presenting the first novel of innovative writers.
Ritual Slaughter is the second book in this series

RITUAL SLAUGHTER

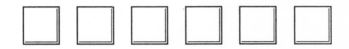

Sharon DRACHE

QUARRY PRESS

The publisher thanks The Canada Council, the Ontario Arts
Council, and the Ministry of Multiculturalism and Citizenship
for assistance in publishing this book.

The author thanks Roger Camm, Arthur Drache, Deborah Drache,
Margaret Dyment, Louis Greenspan, Naim Kattan, Diane Keating,
Jack Hodgins, Joe Rosenblatt, Donn Kushner, Robert Harlow, and
Reuben Slonim for their advice. Special thanks to the Ministry of
Multiculturalism and Citizenship, as well as the Ontario Arts
Council, for financial assistance.

An exerpt from *Ritual Slaughter* appeared
in *Exile* magazine in Spring 1987.

Ritual Slaughter is a work of fiction;
all characters and situations are imaginary.

CANADIAN CATALOGUING IN PUBLICATION DATA

Drache, Sharon, 1943–
Ritual Slaughter
(New Canadian novelists series)
ISBN 0-919627-27-7
1. Jews — Quebec (Province) — Montreal — Fiction.
2. Montreal (Quebec) — Ethnic relations — Fiction.
I. Title. II. Series.
PS8557.R273R48 1989   C813'.54   C89-090008-6
PR9199.3.D73R48 1989

Cover art "Art and Society: *Tout en Cherchant*" by Andre Bieler,
from the permanent collection of the Agnes Etherington Art Centre,
Queen's University, Kingston, Ontario.
Photo documentation by VIDA/Saltmarche, Toronto.

Imaging by ECW Production Services, Sydenham, Ontario.
Printed and bound by Hignell Printing Limited, Winnipeg, Manitoba.

Distributed by University of Toronto Press,
5201 Dufferin Street, Downsview, Ontario M3H 5T8

Published by *Quarry Press, Inc.*,
P.O. Box 1061, Kingston, Ontario K7L 4Y5.

DATSCHLAVER HASIDIM

Rebbe Shlomo Yitzchak Kasarkofski
(b. 1682 Datschlav, Poland)

Shmuel Kasarkofski
(b. 1882 Datschlav, Poland)

Yakov Kasarkofski
(b. 1884 Datschlav, Poland)

Reb Moses *(b. 1902)*
Datschlaver Rebbe of
Williamsburg, New York

Reb Eliahu *(b. 1905)*
Datschlaver Rebbe of
Jerusalem, Isreal

Reb Benjamin *(b. 1904)*
Datschlaver Rebbe
of London, England

Reb Mendel Yehudah *(b. 1916)*
Datschlaver Rebbe of
Montreal, Quebec

Frima *(daughter)*
Shaindel *(daughter)*
Rifkeh *(daughter)*
Rachel *(daughter)*

Mendel Yehudah Kasarkofski, the
Grand Rebbe of the Canadian
Datschlaver Hasidim, decreed:
"It is not for show."

Part
ONE

1

His people hadn't changed. They cared so little for the look of things.

For a long time he lingered outside the corner grocery store, staring uncomfortably across the street at the Hasidic synagogue, a shabby, dilapidated building that didn't look at all like a house of worship. The crooked, weatherbeaten sign above the door traced out in the Yiddish characters *Shtiebel Datschlaver*. Several men in black overcoats and wide-brimmed black hats trimmed with fur stood in a huddle to one side of the front porch. A woman wearing a black, floor-length cape, her head covered by a black scarf, also waited, seated on a grey wooden bench. The men, deliberately keeping their distance from her, disturbed him. Fifteen years had passed since he lived among these people.

Bartholomew had agreed to return to Montreal only because Fiona Shields, his lover, was having a retrospective of her watercolours and sculpture at the *Gallerie Huit Heures* on Sherbrooke. Earlier that morning after breakfast at Ben's with Fiona and *Huit Heures'* curator Danny Wintrob, he had rather hesitantly set out for a walk along the streets of his youth. He walked up Sherbrooke, the cold wind nipping at his cheeks. Not until he turned north on St. Laurent did he feel the fresh warmth of the October sun. After taking an hour to reach the familiar corner of Jeanne Mance and Fairmount, he stopped to look in the window of the grocery where he had first met Fiona.

He could see her standing there behind the horse-shoe shaped lunch counter that took up half the front of the store.

She had thick auburn hair tied in a single braid which trailed to her hips. A pink, billowy, cotton skirt matched a peasant blouse, the transparency revealing her half-cupped, lace brassiere. She no longer dressed like this. In the last five years she had single-mindedly turned to the art of slimming. Now she wore tight, dark-coloured velvet or suede pants with pastel silk blouses, the top buttons always open. "The whole world can see down there," he had complained. "Tolly" (she liked to call him "Tolly" because he was twelve inches taller than her), "I want to show the world that I've got more than height," she'd tease. She was the type of woman who lived openly. Even her paintings revealed this willingness to share.

After her parents had retired to Israel, Fiona lived alone at the back of the grocery in a studio apartment she rented from the new owner. Fanny and Harry Shields had owned and operated this small business for twenty-five years before they decided to leave Canada in 1964. They had begged Fiona to join them, but she insisted on staying in Montreal. "It's time I dedicated myself to my art," she had announced. She told her parents she was nineteen. Free. They, however, did not need reminding. Having hoped their daughter would marry at eighteen, she was already a year overdue. Her wanting a career caused them genuine anxiety. Fiona, however, seemed determined, beginning an apprenticeship to Nicholas Guccini, a sculptor who taught the lost wax method of bronze casting. Every time Fanny and Harry tried to persuade her to abandon her creative ambitions, she produced another critical work. It was as if their opposition fed her talent.

For almost a year before he met Fiona, Bartholomew had been planning his own rebellion for art's sake. He would flee his home in the Hasidic town of Datschlav and change his Datschlaver name, Baruch, to Bartholomew. He made his decision to leave the same evening he learned that he and his betrothed, Frima Kasarkofski, the eldest daughter of the grand rebbe, Mendel Yehudah, were to be married within a year. Oblivious to his feelings, his mother had boasted, *"Ribonu shel Olam* blesses this union. A scholar you aren't, yet the rebbe chooses you."

Already, Mendel Yehudah had confided to Baruch's father, Judah Leib, that even though Frima was his own flesh and blood, a child of the Kasarkofski dynasty, she was guileless, a veritable hayseed among sophisticated humankind, who stumbled constantly over her Yiddish lessons and even her Hebrew prayers. Yet she had a good heart and, most important, a Datschlaver's soul. "An ideal match for your Baruch. He won't object to the gaps in her knowledge for he, himself, knows nothing."

For many years, the rebbe, who had four daughters, but, alas, no sons, grieved over not having a male child to carry on the Kasarkofski court in Canada. He became embittered, resigned to inviting one of his nephews from abroad to succeed him when he passed on. During Baruch's early childhood, the rebbe had hoped that one day he might adopt the son of Judah Leib, the ritual slaughterer. At seven he could shape the letters of the Hebrew alphabet as magnificently as a mature scribe. Mendel Yehudah wished to train the boy for this holy occupation. But he could see that Baruch had no control over his pen. People kept popping up amid his beautifully executed letters on the Torah parchment. The rebbe truly believed that a demon controlled Baruch, like the demon that surely possessed his intellectually limited daughter. Unilaterally, he decided that the two jinxed progeny should live out their lives together. Why contaminate other members of the sect? The proposed match was a compromise, the first in an inexorable chain of decrees, peculiar to the Canadian Datschlavers. In his spare time, Baruch was permitted to draw, a tabu pursuit among Hasidim. The rebbe himself ordered sketching paper and pencils. Even paints and canvases. No longer did Baruch have to resort to creating on the rough parchment used for the holy Torah scrolls. He was officially granted time to produce graven images. The only condition imposed by Mendel Yehudah was that he keep his completed work in a locked room in the rebbe's own house.

No one knew about this unprecedented indulgence except Baruch's immediate family, the rebbe and the rebbetzin. An artist without an audience, he began to doubt his work's existence. He complained bitterly to Mendel Yehudah who repeatedly gave him the same reply: "It is not for show!" At a very young age, Baruch began to feel like the devil incarnate.

One day in the Jeanne Mance grocery, before he bought the Yiddish papers, *The Eagle* and *The Forward*, Baruch had taken his sweet time reading the front pages of *La Presse* and *The Gazette*, papers proscribed by his co-religionists. There were no other customers in the store, and Fiona, who usually was very busy serving meals at the counter, sat on a nearby stool, sipping ginger-ale while she read *The Village Voice*.

Eager to take in as much worldly information as possible in the few minutes before his drive back to Datschlav, he stared over her shoulder on to the art page she was reading. She looked up for a moment catching his dark, brown eyes with hers. "You are interested in art?" she asked. Ashamed, Baruch looked quickly away, reaching into his pocket for the correct change for the Yiddish newspapers.

He bowed, keeping his head down. "Why so formal?" she asked. Baruch stuffed the papers into his canvas bag, fumbling as he tightened the straps and fastened the buckles. Fiona smiled coyly. He wanted desperately to stay and talk with her but instead he nodded stiffly, rushing out of the store to his van parked in front of the Datschlaver synagogue.

As usual he was back at the grocery the following morning and afternoon. With each visit he miraculously managed to exchange a few more sentences with Fiona, although talking with a woman who was not your mother or sister was forbidden in the community. Baruch felt emboldened. He was able to concentrate better on his drawing and painting, which he pursued in the late afternoons and early evenings while the other Datschlaver men studied at the *yeshiva*. He would never be like them. He was not interested in disputing interminable interpretations of Datschlaver law, day after day. Getting to know Fiona brought him great joy but still filled him with ambivalence about his future, particularly his arranged marriage to a woman he did not love.

On many occasions he had expressed his dislike for the match and had angered his mother. "The rebbe is doing you both a favour. What will become of you, if you don't obey?" The more Baruch contemplated life in Datschlav with Frima Kasarkofski as his wife, the more miserable and restless he became.

One afternoon, following a month of his friendly visits with Fiona, she invited him to her studio apartment at the back of the grocery store. She gave him a glass of tea and a slice of bread with homemade apricot jam. Baruch impulsively embraced her. Tensing with excitement, he fondled her like an abandoned animal. Fiona snuggled against his black gaberdine. She unbuttoned his white cotton shirt and placed her warm face against his bare chest.

The van left at the regular time for the trip back to Datschlav. Baruch, however, did not show up. Simon Krakower, the synagogue beadle, had to drive. The following day, Baruch decided that he would never return to his community. He trimmed his soft, long beard, forming it into a perfect triangle, and he discarded his black capote, black hat, and even his fringed undergarment. Today, at last, he was heading home.

The same, familiar beadle opened the door. In English, he asked, "What do you want by us? Services are over . . . finished . . . understand?"

Bartholomew smiled as he heard the quaint insertion of the word *by*. The Datschlavers often inserted this preposition before proper names or pronouns when they spoke English instead of their usual Yiddish.

"Please," Bartholomew requested, "I would like to go to Datschlav for the day."

The beadle sternly addressed him, "Why? You got business? We don't let strangers visit, unless they're expected." He paused. "Wait a minute. I'll get the book." He went over to the hall table, returning with a bulky ledger. Consulting the day's list which the rebbetzin had dictated on the phone the evening before, he asked bluntly, "Name?"

"Why do you want my name?"

"It's very simple. If your name is not on the list, you can't go," the man grumbled.

"Bartholomew Bessette."

"H–m–m . . . Bartholomew Bessette?" Krakower repeated, raising his eyes to study him. *"Ribonu shel Olam*, it cannot be," he said. "Is it possible that you are not Bartholomew Bessette but Baruch Berkovitch, the son of Judah Leib, the slaughterer, and the good Rebeccah Leah?"

The woman seated on the bench who had silently followed their conversation could no longer restrain herself. "Baruch! Baruch!" she cried out. In her excitement her head scarf fell off. Baruch thought he recognized her, but he was so repelled by her shorn scalp he could not believe she was his eldest sister, Faigele. When he had last seen her, she wore her thick, black hair in an extravagant chignon. Fifteen years ago, the Hasidic village had buzzed with the sacrilege of Faigele Berkovitch: unmarried at twenty-three, a wicked non-conformist. Just like her brother.

Gradually, the community had learned that Baruch, instead of applying himself to *yeshiva* studies, had filled his days with sketching and drawing. He remembered his father, Judah Leib, weeping in the presence of Mendel Yehudah who nodded compassionately as he swayed in prayer. It seemed that the rebbe was always praying or poring over *Dinim*, the Datschlaver commentary of laws and customs. For Baruch's own particular aberration, his love of creation, the rebbe had consulted several sacred texts.

"Perhaps," he told Judah Leib, *"Ribonu shel Olam* decrees a different destiny for your son." He reminded the slaughterer that as an infant Baruch had crawled backwards. "A sign," Mendel Yehudah had proclaimed even then, advising Judah

Leib and Rebeccah Leah to try to have another son. Despite fasting and prayer by his father, fate winked in the other direction and Baruch was indeed the last offspring born after his sisters, Faigele, Sara, Bryna, and Hannah.

With the founding of Datschlav in 1963, Baruch began to travel daily to Montreal, driving commuting Datschlavers to and from the city, delivering Yiddish newspapers to the rebbe only, picking up bread baked especially for the Datschlavers at the kosher bakery on St. Viatur. Keeping the young artist busy seemed like the best plan to the rebbe. Again and again he begged Baruch to repent, yet in private he encouraged him to dream and draw. Although Baruch was baffled by his behaviour towards him, he never once questioned the rebbe's inconsistency.

Faigele held her hands up to cover her head while Baruch reached for her kerchief. He tried to conceal his feelings. Looking steadily into her eyes, he asked, "How are Mother and Father?"

"My dear brother," she whispered demurely, securing the scarf at the back of her head. "I see you have not heard the sad news . . . our beloved father has passed on. The funeral is today."

"Our father is dead?" he muttered in disbelief, tears he had thought he was incapable of filling his eyes. "What happened, Faigele? He was only fifty-seven."

"It was an accident. On the kill floor . . . "

"Come on, not Papa," Baruch interrupted. "He was far too good at his work to have an accident."

"No one understands," she started to cry.

Baruch looked out to the street. The Datschlaver van, the very same vehicle he travelled in years ago, pulled up. They keep everything forever, he mused to himself. The chauffeur, a young man in a McGill jacket, got out. Krakower, the beadle, called out to him as he pointed at Faigele and Baruch: "The regular group and two extra, Abe Tarnow's wife and the stranger."

"I'm sorry I haven't asked you about your family," Baruch apologized, "but the news of our father's death has shaken me ... How is your husband? And your children?" He fixed his eyes on Faigele's kerchiefed head. "You must have many children?"

"Only two," she replied. "The rebbe says, I, like you, have a different destiny."

"Dearest Faigele ... " Baruch touched his sister's shoulder. Krakower approached, patting Baruch on the back like a long, lost brother. "Sorry, my friend that we meet under such unfortunate circumstances. Your father was a good man." Then, changing his tone of voice, the beadle ogled Baruch's clothes as though they carried the plague itself. "Where on earth did you get that outfit?"

"The Village in New York," Baruch answered nervously. Perhaps he shouldn't have come back, he thought, especially dressed like this, but he needed to show, not merely tell, how far he had come from his past.

He watched Krakower adjust his black fedora so that his bushy sidelocks pushed presumptuously forward. A faithful Datschlaver, born and raised in Montreal, the farthest he had ever travelled was to Datschlav.

Beside him, Baruch felt awkward, dressed in his favourite rabbit fur jacket, the sleeves trimmed with mauve leather. Mauve kid gloves and a mauve mohair scarf completed his unusual costume. Unusual compared to the dark, baggy clothing of the regular commuters. Baruch's head was uncovered, his black hair cut short. His goatee and bushy moustache were other physical characteristics separating him from the members of the sect to which he had once belonged. All the Datschlaver men had flowing beards and sidelocks, one whose were so long he braided them. Baruch resented the braids because they belonged to this young man, while his sister, since her marriage, had no hair. In Datschlav, wigs, like female hair, were considered immodest and therefore categorically forbidden, except on the Sabbath and other holidays when one could let oneself relax and enjoy the company of one's spouse. The Hasid with the elegant braids wore braces on his teeth, his single concession to the twentieth century. Baruch watched the way he delighted in shaping his mouth into a forced smile.

Since he had abandoned the Hasidic community, he had not made a single phone call to his family. Yet his sister's announcement of his father's unexpected death overwhelmed him with melancholy.

Standing before Faigele, he no longer felt estranged. "I'm more upset by our father's death than I ever thought I could be," he confided, his voice trembling. "But look what has happened to you . . . you used to have such beautiful hair . . . ."

2

The van weaved its way northward through the city on to the autoroute leading away from Montreal. Baruch and Faigele sat together behind the Hasidim. Usually women sat separately, but Baruch was permitted to sit beside his sister since his dress as well as his attitude indicated that he was no longer a follower of his sect. Four rows in front of them were filled, three men in each. With their black coats and broad-rimmed hats, they formed a dark, mysterious barrier. Curious drivers in passing cars peered up at the bright yellow bus with its bold, black lettering in English and Yiddish: *Datschlav, Quebec*.

Just beyond Vanier, at a junction indicating the road for the twin cities of Claremont-Ste Justine, the little bus turned off the autoroute into the service area of an isolated Texaco gas station. The McGill student came to the rear of the vehicle to check the baked goods stored beside Faigele and Baruch.

"What a fuss they'll make if these baskets aren't sealed proper-ly," he complained. "Last week, the wrapping on one of them was loose and the corner of an onion bun slipped into view. I nearly lost my job." Tightening the wax paper and tin foil packaging, he asked Baruch. "What do you think of these Datschlavers?"

"Ask my sister."

"Sorry, I'm not allowed to talk to the good women. Not even to your sister or the rebbetzin. Rules, you know, rules."

"I thought my sister and the rebbetzin were special."

The student snickered. "They're special, all right. I don't mind," he said, "neither does the old lady, but your sister here, she gets a little lonely." He addressed Faigele, in almost a whisper. "You do get lonely sometimes, don't you, sister?"

Faigele looked pleadingly at her brother. Perhaps he would speak on her behalf. But he had been away for so many years. What could he possibly say in her defense?

"You'll see what I mean when we get to Datschlav," the driver nodded. "Won't be long, now." He closed the back door and paid the gas attendant.

Soon they turned on to a winding dirt road. For a few miles Baruch could see only flat land and spruce trees appearing against the low lying Laurentians. But several bends in the road later, the Hasidic village loomed as unexpectedly as ever on the otherwise deserted country road. The community had grown since Baruch had left. There were only thirty-six houses on Datschlav's main street, *Rehov Zion*, then. Baruch counted many more homes, perhaps a hundred, forming a giant square, as formidable as any urban facsimile with a central boulevard enclosed by massive, wrought iron fencing. He could hardly recognize the gardens, planted when the village was estab-lished. Individual hills proffering the rebbe's favourite herbs had spread wildly, each variety bearing a sign in Yiddish: fennel, hyssop, sweet cicely, coriander, and marjoram.

Only a few minutes earlier he had read road signs in French. Mature linden trees, like leafy sentinels, lined the pathways used for pedestrians. Park benches faced cultivated rose gardens bordered by white pansies. Baruch thought the boulevard in its final fall bloom appeared to be the only lavish aspect of the Hasidic town until he saw the yellow stucco *yeshiva*, a modern structure at least four times the size he remembered, and the slaughterhouse, expanded in length and breadth to the size of a city shopping centre. Green pastures flanked the two storey emporium, painted white, trimmed with blue, bearing two signs: *L'abbatoir Datschlav* in yellow, transliterated Yiddish; *Richard Vincennes* in Roman, blue.

The girls' and boys' schools as well as the two buildings housing the ritualaria (one for men and one for women) were yellow stucco, like the holy of holies, the *yeshiva*. In the parking lot beside the slaughterhouse stood a fleet of fifty white trucks, bright crimson curtains hanging in the windows. From the distance, the vertical and horizontal line-up looked to Baruch like a giant cross. He laughed to himself at the absurdity of the Christian image.

"Not the Datschlav you knew, is it?" Faigele asked.

"It's incredible," Baruch answered. "Quite incredible."

"The white trucks, everyone of the fifty is refrigerated," Faigele told him, "and the transports over there, near the slaughterhouse, a hundred of them, all have freezers. You won't believe this, Baruch, but Datschlav delivers *glatt kosher* meat to twenty-seven smaller Jewish communities in Ontario and Quebec." She pointed again to the parking lot. Baruch looked in amazement at the trucks shining in the afternoon sun. "And that's not all," Faigele said, "Those transports carry *treyfe* to cities and towns as far west as Fort William and as far east as Chicoutimi ..."

"So, the Datschlavers must have some money?" Baruch said.

"Money, what do we need money for? We live simply. Look at *Rehov Zion*. Are the homes not as modest as you remember them?"

Baruch had to admit they were. "I don't understand," he said. "You are making much more money than you need. What are you doing with it?"

"Dear brother, do you remember the negotiations with Richard Vincennes when the Datschlavers bought this land?"

"Of course I remember. Months of meetings before Rebbe Mendel Yehudah agreed to let Richard Vincennes remain on his parents' farm to act as a mediator between us and the neighbouring Gentiles."

"But the rebbe wanted Vincennes to keep his distance, to be available only when *we* needed him," Faigele added, stressing *we*. The bus stopped at *Rehov Yakov*. Baruch looked out his window and saw a huge, ivy covered wall.

"That's where he lives," Faigele said. "In a moment, you'll see the house." The bus passed a driveway fringed with meticulously trimmed cedar leading to a grey stone mansion with leaded glass windows. Wrought iron balconies decorated every second floor window and a spacious veranda on the first floor extended into the front garden. Vincenne's home was extraordinarily luxurious compared to the other Datschlaver residences. Looking back at the drab houses and religious buildings on *Rehov Zion* and finally over to the slaughterhouse, Baruch felt wretched and uneasy.

He recalled how his father had tried to teach him the art of the ritual slaughter, how he had insisted that Baruch accompany him to the abbatoir. He could see his father in the basement of their home sharpening his knives on the grey and black whetstones, his father's index finger nail filed especially to test for sharpness. Again and again he passed this nail over the rectangular blades to make sure there was no flaw that could cause the animal pain. He told Baruch: "One day, these knives will be yours ... watch and learn, my son."

He respected his father too much to tell him he would never use the knives. The shining blades would rust were they left to him.

3

The bus pulled up in front of Rebbe Mendel Yehudah Kasar-kofski's house. Because he had been away these many years, Baruch thought he should see the rebbe first to ask permission to return for this short, one day visit.

Frima, the rebbe's eldest daughter and his former betrothed, greeted him at the door. How well he remembered her while she obviously had forgotten him. She had the same buck teeth and persistent acne of her youth. To her added misfortune, she also had several holes marking her face, the result of the grotesque creativity of chicken pox she had suffered as a high strung teenager. But what struck Baruch most was her dark brown head scarf. She was such a homely woman whose best physical attribute had been her curly, blonde hair. Now, he surmised, it was gone. Like his sister and all the other married women, no female was exempt. Frima was as obese as ever, her unkempt bulk contained in a red-flowered dress with long sleeves and a tightly buttoned collar. Each flower had a thin, green stem winding onto its neighbour, forming a vine puffed out by her generous girth. Although she wore black stockings and the skirt of her flowered dress was long, her chubby calves still showed, making her feet look like they were planted only with great difficulty inside her cumbersome oxfords.

Several men already waiting to see the rebbe were seated at the oval dining table at one end of the living room. Frima invited Baruch to join them. Meanwhile, the rebbe's other daughters, Shaindel, Rifkeh, and Rachel joined their sister at

the cupboard, giggling fiercely, while their mother, the rebbetzin, strode into the room. A towering individual, she wore a
brown-flowered dress, similar in pattern to Frima's. Her head
scarf, also brown-flowered, had a wide beak projecting over
her forehead. Looking more like a policewoman than a rebbetzin, her scrutinizing eyes and frowning visage added to her
authoritarian arsenal. Scrupulous devotion to Datschlaver
law had honed her naturally superior demeanor and the pad-
ding in the shoulders of her dress further accentuated her
charismatic armour. She feasted her judgmental eyes on the
men gathered about the table before heading directly for the
rebbe's office.

Although she made Baruch feel very nervous, he took advantage of her absence to study the room he had not seen for so
long. Still the same white, Italian provincial furniture
trimmed with gold: the tables crowded with ornate china,
painted with romantic pastoral scenes, totally inconsistent
with the Datschlaver way of life. Their rigid philosophy didn't
blend with this middle class decor. He stared at the floral
appliqué cut velvet six-seater sofa and each of the four matching chairs covered with clear plastic. He could see the silver
zippers running up the sides of each piece of furniture holding the covers in place. The room was so full that one could
pass through only by careful, painstaking navigation. Baruch,
of course, knew that the furnishings and other ornaments
were gifts to the rebbe and his wife in appreciation for their
services, honouring the rebbe's abilities as faith healer and
miracle worker.

A plastic runner going from the hall to the dining table and
a second runner extending from the rebbetzin's chair at the
head of the table to the rebbe's office already bore the brown
smudges of the day's traffic. (The streets of Datschlav were
not paved.) Under the table, a red-flowered rug completed the
unharmonious decor.

After a quarter of an hour the rebbetzin returned with a
ledger similar to but larger than Krakower's. She placed it on

the white damask cloth which was covered with clear plastic like the sofa and chairs. In the middle of the table sat a large comporte of aqua porcelain, the plate part supported by three plump cherubim which was itself filled with waxy fruit. She opened her book and began taking attendance.

"Meir Rabinovitch."

"Present."

"Please write here what you wish to discuss with the rebbe," she droned.

Rabinovitch, a seedy looking chap, wearing a blood-stained apron, stood up. "*Nu!* What should I write? I've come about the kill."

The rebbetzin ran her index finger down an open page. Raising her pudgy palm, she pointed at Rabinovitch. "Wait a minute, mister," she said. "Let me see your hands."

Sheepishly he held them out, his fingernails caked with dried blood, the skin stained with reddish-brown blotches.

"I'll write," announced Rebbetzin. "How many minutes, Rabinovitch?"

"Ten, maybe fifteen at the most."

Rebbetzin carefully recorded the time in her ledger. "Thank you," she nodded. "Moishe Shatsky."

A scrawny man in a navy three piece suit scurried from his seat at the end of the table. Taking Rebbetzin's pen, he wrote, "Gas for the lorries. *Five minutes.*" Hastily bowing to avoid eye contact with the rebbetzin, his yarmulke flew as though a mischievous imp had propelled it from his head on to her lap. The lady jumped to her feet, standing so quickly that her chair fell over. Shatsky rushed to pick up his cap which had fallen to the floor and to restore her chair to its upright position. The flustered rebbetzin sat down again to resume her roll call. "Reb Lazare Lichtenstein."

Reb Lazare wore traditional garb, a black brocade waistcoat, a satin *shtriemel* trimmed with red fox. When Rebbetzin called his name, he stood slowly, taking off his broad fur-trimmed hat, placing it on the table. Still, his head was covered with a white crocheted skull cap. Two gold and silver tassels in the centre caught the noon sun streaming through the living room window.

Reb Lichtenstein silently paced the distance of the oval dining table before he gave his answer. With his eyes fixed on the men, first Meir Rabinovitch, next Moishe Shatsky, he actually dared to stand so close to the rebbetzin that he could whisper in her ear.

Delighted with himself, he stood back, checking his own black book which he took out of his waistcoat pocket. "Thirty minutes," he repeated aloud to everyone present. Feverishly he computed costs for cattle shipments from Passover to the Jewish New Year. "That includes time to discuss the Manitoba shipment," he added.

Not many Datschlavers were allowed such a lengthy audience with the rebbe. Shaking Reb Lazare's hand, Moishe Shatsky curled his thick lips upward in approval. Rebbetzin sighed, taking a deep breath. It was time to address the stranger.

"Monsieur," she said to him, "Your name, please."

"Bartholomew Bessette," he replied.

Humph, she thought. Certainly not a Jewish name. Who is he? What does he want with Rebbe? Strangers are usually accompanied by Richard Vincennes and they sit quietly while he speaks on their behalf. For instance, the municipal tax collector, Monsieur Blanchette from Claremont-Ste Justine, Vincennes speaks for him. But this stranger pranced in here as if there were no question about his right to speak alone with the rebbe. "I won't allow such impertinence," Baruch heard her mutter.

She rubbed her chin where several grey hairs sprouted and strained her half closed eyes (no woman worth her Datschlav salt ever looked directly at a male unless he was younger than thirteen) to study his face, announcing candidly to those assembled, "Looks Jewish, this stranger! Monsieur," she at last said to him, "What is your business in Datschlav? The rebbe, he only speaks to Jewish people. Understand?"

"I am a Jew."

"Ah, you have changed your name? You are for some good reason a self deprecator? But look at you, the way you are dressed ... certainly you are not an Hasid ... are you really Jewish?"

Baruch nodded, glowering proudly. "Inside I am a Jew." And yes, he thought to himself, I do dress differently, but look at them, in black from head to toe, with the exception of the red fox trimming their hats. Dull conformists ... anti-life ... joy haters. Their women in sexless, grey dresses are gawking mischievously at me from the hall. Only Frima and her mother dress differently, although grey would suit them too. Their baggy, flowered dresses are even uglier than the drab, joyless garments that the other women are wearing.

Baruch adjusted his green serge tunic, abruptly tugging at the long cape sleeves trimmed with rabbit fur. Rebbetzin, occupied with consulting time slots for the day's audiences with Rebbe, cast a furtive glance away from her ledger, resting her gaze on his thick mauve sash, tied loosely about his waist. From the sash's macramé tassels swung at least a dozen rabbit's feet. The man was mad ... an alien ... certainly not a believer. She concluded that his eyes were not centered properly and that he might even be a murderer. Agonizing about what he could possibly want from her husband, she decided to conduct a preliminary investigation before granting him an audience.

"Maybe you'd like something to eat, Mister? A glass of tea, perhaps?" The stranger's eating habits might yield some important clue about his character. Rebbetzin prided herself as a wonderful hostess. She had already served the other three men, happily sipping from their glasses of tea with floating slices of lemon and enjoying the accompanying poppyseed cookies. Reb Lazare dunked his expertly in his tea.

"I baked them myself," she said proudly. "You should eat, Mister, after your trip. Such a trip." She raised her eyebrows.

What trip? He had travelled only twenty miles north of Montreal. Besides, he'd had breakfast at Ben's that morning, not to mention the meal Danny Wintrob had treated him to the night before in the Maritime Bar at the Ritz Carleton: *soupe à la tortue, scampi au pernod, salade romaine avec petits morceaux de bacon* . . . .

"You eat kosher, Mister?"

He felt a lump rise in his throat. He could lie to her. "After a fashion," he hedged, awkwardly.

"So, you're not hungry, then?"

He knew she suspected him the moment he walked through her front hall into her living room. Datschlavers were trained to smell trouble and *treyfe*, especially *treyfe apikorsim*. But suddenly her grimace softened. He watched her smile for the first time since she had begun her questioning.

"*Ribonu shel Olam.* Is it possible that you are Baruch Berkovitch, the son of Judah Leib, the slaughterer, *olav-ha-shalom* and the good Rebeccah Leah?"

Baruch nervously stroked his moustache. "Yes," he said and hoped that would end it.

"I didn't recognize you," Rebbetzin said cooly. "Well, look at you . . . how could I?"

"I am an artist, Rebbetzin," he replied. For himself, his vocation provided sufficient explanation. He chose not to tell her about his teaching position at Columbia. Revealing that he taught art history at that secular institution would baffle her even more than if he told that in the fifteen years since he had left Datschlav he had nurtured his art and neglected his religion. Obsessed with the thought of impressing her, he took out his mauve leather satchel from behind the rabbit fur bobbing back and forth on his jacket sleeve. "Would you care to see my creations?" he bravely asked.

Rebbetzin's face turned crimson and her voice grew tense and strained. "I cannot look at your art, Baruch. You know it is forbidden."

Reb Lazare closed the commentary he had been studying and

announced. "I'll wait in the front hall until the idolater leaves."

Meir Rabinovitch and Moishe Shatsky frantically nodded their heads in agreement. The three men marched out of the room, their hands shielding their eyes. In the vestibule, they stood facing the front door, Meir Rabinovitch engrossed in his recitation of Psalms, Moishe Shatsky rechecking his accounts, and Reb Lazare resuming his chanting of the Datschlaver commentary on the weekly Torah portion.

Baruch waited until they appeared settled before he continued. "I see custom has not altered in my absence. Art is still considered pagan. Come, Madam, surely if I tell you that I am a successful, highly acclaimed artist, I must stimulate your curiosity. We're alone now. You really ought to have a look."

Rebbetzin shrugged. "I suppose it wouldn't hurt if I were to take a peek." She had seen her husband, the grand rebbe, take plenty, closeting himself in the locked room where he had ordered Baruch to store his paintings and drawings when he lived in the community. He often told the rebbetzin that he had felt compelled to control Baruch, but an unusual look of satisfaction mixed with pleasure lurked behind his mask of concern. Once he had admitted to her that Baruch's art was shocking and unnatural. When she asked him to explain further, he provided the customary reply: "It is not for show!"

With trembling hands he wiped his perspiring forehead with his handkerchief before he removed his pictures from his satchel, carefully spreading them on the table. Pictures of Hasidim! Men and women, together!

In one picture nearly fifty gathered in a large circle around a Christmas tree. Each person, including the women, dressed in modern, fashionable clothing carried a Torah. The women's kerchiefs covered only have their shorn heads. The rebbetzin shook her head in dismay, and he hastily began to pick up his portraits until she stopped him. "May I see another of your pictures, Baruch?"

Deliberately, he chose a painting in which there were just as many Hasidim, but this time they were naked, absolutely, except for the men's *striemels* trimmed with red fox and the women's multi-coloured head scarves. Baruch had drawn only the backs of the Hasidim, the men's bottom slim, the women's fat and saggy.

Rebbetzin screamed when she saw this picture. Her daughters came running from the hall where they had been eavesdropping. "What is it, Mama?"

"Put those graven images away immediately," she yelled at Baruch. "Don't look," she hastened to warn her daughters. "Don't look or the Evil Eye will take hold."

Baruch put his pictures back in his satchel. An uncomfortable silence filled the room until the rebbetzin chose to break it. "Look who has returned," she exclaimed, "Baruch Berkovitch, the son of the good Rebeccah Leah and the slaughterer, Judah Leib *olav-ha-shalom!*"

"Ah, Judah Leib!" the girls sang out, "It is good he is not here to see this shame. It would kill him!"

Baruch could not resist. "You did say *olav-ha-shalom*, Rebbetzin? My father is dead, is he not?"

His father was dead, but now he remembered that for these devout Datschlavers, his father was not really dead but merely on his journey to *The World To Come*.

He watched Rebbetzin stroke the hair on her chin before she confronted him. "Is it wise that your mother should see you? Look at the way you are dressed. And your hair, with no sidelocks. Surely you will upset her?"

"With all due respect, Rebbetzin, I am her only son and isn't a son, even a rebellious one, a comfort to his mother?"

The rebbetzin sighed. "This is definitely a question for the rebbe."

"I would like to see the rebbe," Baruch assured her, "to ask permission to visit here today. Perhaps, for *shiva* too," he added. Rebbetzin's daughters examined Baruch as if he were an intriguing, modern monster. They deluged him with questions while the men in the vestibule continued to ignore him. Frima, the eldest began: "Mister, why do you wear a dress?"

Baruch replied simply, "I wear whatever I feel like wearing."

"You choose your own clothes?" Frima asked in disbelief, turning to the rebbetzin. "Mama, how is it possible? *Ribonu shel Olam* will surely punish this Evil Doer?"

"Baruch is no longer one of us," the rebbetzin replied. "He is only a visitor."

"Yes, Mama," she acknowledged like an obedient child.

There was no open recognition of Baruch as her former betrothed. Only a bland, formal acceptance of her mother's explanation. Baruch attributed her apathy to her simple-mindedness as well as to the general apathy of Datschlaver women accustomed to accepting unconditionally all that was said to them by their superiors, usually men, but in this case, the rebbetzin.

Shaindel, Rifkeh, and Rachel raced to the kitchen, each returning with a plate of her own baking.

"Cinnamon buns with raisins. I baked them myself . . . try one, Mister," Shaindel said breathlessly. Rifkeh chimed in, "Wouldn't you like some of my honey cake baked just this morning?"

Baruch wanted to be courteous but he wasn't hungry. Once again he refused all food offered to him.

"You'll be weak if you don't eat. You should eat, Mister," urged Frima.

Rebbetzin hustled to Rebbe's office to tell him the news. She returned to announce, "The rebbe will see you first, Baruch Berkovitch." In the presence of the pious men, the beak of her head scarf cutting his cheek, she whispered, "It's good to have you home, my boy." Since her brief consultation with the rebbe, her attitude had changed. There were still some miracles, Baruch decided.

4

The rebbe's office was exactly as Baruch remembered. Grey, bare walls with small, high windows. No furniture except for a long, oak, pedestal table covered by a white cloth, fleshed over with the usual, clear plastic and two rows of matching chairs lined up along one side of the room.

Rebbe Mendel Yehudah sat alone at the head of the table. His white beard spilled over his chin, descending to his waist and a prayershawl covering his head cascaded down the sides of his body. *Dinim*, a book of laws and teachings of the first Datschlaver rebbe, Shlomo Yitzchak Kasarkofski, born in Poland in the seventeenth century, lay on the sparse table and also a black telephone. As he sat bent over his reading, the rebbe appeared shrunken, much older than this sixty-four years.

No sooner had Baruch and the rebbetzin entered the room than the phone rang. The rebbe merely nodded and she immediately fetched two chairs, placing one close to the rebbe, and the other, halfway down the table, for Baruch.

He watched the rebbe speak softly into the receiver, first in Yiddish, then switching to English. "Give me the child's father . . . yes, in Newcastle-on-Tyne." He paused, momentarily gazing up at the ceiling, as if he were searching for inspiration. "So," he continued, "he thinks I am going to perform miracles right here in this room. Some secretary, I have," he muttered.

Baruch learned that Solomon Lifsky, the rebbe's secretary, screened all incoming calls, briefing Mendel Yehudah as soon as he picked up the phone. The rebbe listened intently. Within seconds he began swaying in prayer, invoking the name of the young boy from Newcastle-on-Tyne. The phone gripped in one hand, he suddenly broke off from Hebrew to Yiddish, saying, should the child, *Ribonu shel Olam* forbid, die, he would certainly be giving up this world for *The World To Come*, an incorruptible world where the archangel, Gabriel, would personally cater to his every whim, where the child would patiently await his parents and the chosen of the house of Israel. "It is the will of our father in heaven," said the rebbe, yet, he still advised the parents to try to have another child. He terminated this portion of the conversation by blowing three shrill notes on his ram's horn, which he kept tucked inside the folds of his caftan. Baruch assumed he even slept with the instrument. It was always with him. Because the rebbe had unwittingly turned up the amplifier on his phone receiver, a device he relied upon when he wished to share his phone calls with visitors, Baruch could hear Solomon Lifsky offer particular advice to the parents of the sick boy. "You are to follow Plan C on page one hundred and sixty-two of *Dinim*." Baruch actually began venerating the team.

"Have you heard the news, Rebbe?" Lifsky continued, "Our Baruch Berkovitch is back ... and on the very day of Judah Leib's funeral."

"I know, he is here in my study. Hold all calls, Lifsky," he replied in an ominous tone which appeared to take on a quaver for Baruch's sake. Ever so slowly, the rebbe removed his prayershawl, folding it carefully, totally engrossed in the activity. A small skull cap resting on his long white hair shifted.

How wan his face was. Like the pages of a rare, old book, Baruch thought. He decided he would paint the rebbe in this room when he returned to New York. But now, he was satisfied to draw in his mind: the rebbe and *Dinim*, the Datschlaver Law, indistinguishable from one another. He'd have a huge canvas, worthy of his idea.

For the first time since he had stepped into his office, the rebbe addressed him. "You still speak Yiddish?" he asked.

"Of course," Baruch replied, "I haven't forgotten everything."

The rebbe again nodded to his wife, "So, you will leave us. Baruch and I must speak alone." The rebbe directed him to sit in the rebbetzin's abandoned chair. Having never sat so close to the master, he began to perspire profusely. He found himself awkwardly saying, "I'm sorry, Rebbe, for returning at such a sad time. My father's death has come as a great shock to me."

"Do not apologize, Baruch. You did not come of your own volition," he paused. "My informants have kept me in touch with your activities since you left the community. I know you have worked very hard to develop your talent. I have always hoped you would succeed."

"Thank you, Rebbe," he said, squirming in his chair. "You were always interested in what you called 'my artistic deviation.'"

"I did call it that, didn't I." A smile crossed his face. "Your work, though I never approved of it, gave me profound pleasure. I felt compelled to encourage you to draw and paint. You must understand it was not easy for me, in the same way that it was not easy for me to indulge your sister."

"But why?" he asked the rebbe, who was obviously growing impatient, a characteristic Baruch recalled always surfaced when the master felt he had disclosed more than he should. Yet he continued. "Your father, *olav-ha-shalom*, was partly responsible. He also was always drawn to the ways of the world."

"But now he is gone and I, too, am out of the picture. Only Faigele remains. Does this please you?"

The rebbe stared into and through the telephone as if he were willing it to ring, in spite of his previous request to Solomon Lifsky not to put through any calls. "My sister," he repeated to the rebbe. "What about my sister?"

"Ah, Faigele," he sighed, "she has always been such a beauty. With her I had to make an exception."

"An exception?" asked Baruch. "To me she looks exactly like all the other Datschlaver women."

"What she is on the outside has absolutely nothing to do with the inner Faigele," he protested. "You know the philosophy of the community, Baruch? You remember the rules?"

"Yes, Rebbe, I remember." Only too well, he thought to himself. Perhaps he had stayed long enough. "Rebbe, I think it best that I leave Datschlav as soon as possible. But I would like to stay for my father's funeral."

"Yes, Baruch, you must stay for the funeral but you should also remain for the week of mourning." Rebbe stroked his long, white beard. He adjusted his skull cap. Baruch could see he was troubled. "Do you remember the French Canadian, Richard Vincennes?" the rebbe asked.

"Of course, I remember him. He was the first person from outside the community to see my work. He believed in my talent and he told me so."

"Yes," the rebbe nodded, "Richard Vincennes admires," he paused, "*Ribonu shel Olam* should forgive me for saying . . . *art*. He also admires the Datschlavers." He paused again. "*Ribonu shel Olam* should also forgive me for mentioning *art* in the same breath as I mention our people. Richard Vincennes is also dedicated to Datschlav."

"Ten years ago," the rebbe continued, "when we were just beginning to make money in this town because of the slaughterhouse, I set up a trust fund with your father and Mr. Vincennes as the sole trustees. Our community's savings were tucked away in both their names to accumulate interest for the Datschlavers."

In *The World To Come*, Baruch thought to himself as he glanced about the spartan office.

"Every year, Mr. Vincennes has received payment from the trust fund in return for services rendered to Datschlav, but to the day he died, your father never took a penny of the money to which he was legally entitled.

"What I am about to tell you, Baruch, will be, as it was to

33

me, an even greater revelation. Just yesterday, the notary from Claremont-Ste Justine called here asking for you. It appears your father has named you trustee under his will."

"*Ribonu shel Olam*," cried Baruch, "I am trustee for Datschlav, proud owner of money that can never be touched."

"We must ensure the safety of our community," the rebbe merely shrugged. "If Richard Vincennes wishes to live like a rich man, let him, but for we Datschlavers to be even comfortable is out of the question. What do we need trouble for?" the rebbe groaned, clearing his throat before swallowing. "Datschlav is a charitable organization. Since the community's inception, we have not paid a penny of municipal, provincial, or federal tax. Mr. Vincennes, on the other hand, is master of his own affairs."

"What would you like me to do, Rebbe?"

"You're asking, so I shall tell you. Sign over your trusteeship to Faigele. Leave the money in Datschlav, where it belongs, or move back here, yourself, and remain trustee in your father's place."

"You make it sound so simple, but I cannot change my life with a moment's notice."

"Not so long ago, you did precisely that, Baruch Berkovitch." The rebbe had not lost his touch for inducing guilt.

"Not really, my decision to leave Datschlav did take time. For years I brooded about my departure from this sect. Perhaps, when I first started to draw. I was seven, remember?"

"Yes, I remember very well."

Baruch did not want to dwell on the past. Enough of it he acknowledged by his return. He refused to be squeezed into a corner, bribed with money. "Before I make up my mind about your generous offer, I must speak with my sister and Richard Vincennes. But I assure you, Rebbe, I have chosen my path. I am dedicated to art, not to religion or money, and I'm certainly not a thief. I, too, would rather see the money where it belongs," he found himself hesitating, "with the Datschlavers."

34

The rebbe nodded eagerly. "Bless you. I knew you would see your father's mistake. All income earned by the Datschlavers is meant to be saved in perpetuity."

"I understand," said Baruch, "but don't you think your people ought to spend some of their precious savings. Look at the way Vincennes lives while Datschlav's streets, except for the pathways on the boulevards, aren't even paved. Your homes are too small for the number of people living in them. The kitchen and bathroom facilities are inadequate. 'A shame!' " Baruch declared, invoking one of the Datschlaver's favourite, judgmental expressions.

"I have already explained why we must live modestly," the rebbe said. "You will understand more if you stay with us for awhile. So much has happened since you left the community."

"Yes, so much," Baruch said sadly, the thought of his father's death foremost in his mind. "Perhaps I will stay for a few weeks," he volunteered. "We do have a lot of business, don't we, Rebbe?"

"By all means, stay as long as you like."

"First I'll have to get in touch with Fiona . . . "

"Fiona Shields?" the rebbe interrupted him. He had never approved of that woman. "How she broke her parents' hearts," he muttered aloud. "Fanny and Harry Shields are good people. Even Orthodox," he added. "But Fiona has always brought them *tsures*. How is she?" the rebbe asked reproachfully.

"Couldn't be better. In fact, she's a huge success. We came to Montreal for a retrospective of her paintings and sculpture."

"Shocking!" the rebbe replied, reluctantly acknowledging her reputation as an artist. "Simply shocking!"

"But Rebbe, Fiona is very gifted. She is a great artist."

The rebbe shook his head in dismay. "*Ribonu shel Olam*, what is the world coming to?"

"Look Rebbe, I'll try to be a good Datschlaver while I'm here but the world beyond this community is different. Even the other sects of Hasidim are different from us. You'll forgive me for saying so, but the Datschlaver way of life is narrow in the extreme."

"Yes, Baruch, thank you for giving me your opinion. Now, you must prepare yourself for your father's funeral. I shall summon Abe Tarnow, Faigele's husband. He will take you to the *mikveh*. You must purify yourself. You have been away a long time, Baruch Berkovitch."

5

The water in the ritualarium, siphoned directly from an underground stream, was murky. He hated immersing himself in it because of the uncertain shades of green mixed with brown. However, Abe Tarnow, the *mikveh* supervisor and his brother-in-law, stood by as his official witness.

"Immersion is good for the soul, my friend. See if you can count to thirty and sing *dayenu* when you go under and you'll be ready for a positive judgment at the gates of heaven," he laughed, his thick red beard shaking and his plumose belly rippling beneath his black, silk kimona. He was always making jokes that he enjoyed far more than his listeners. Still, he repeated them to the same bored people who only managed a weak smile.

Extremely embarrassed about his nakedness, Baruch held his towel as tightly as he could over his private parts, while Tarnow passed a soft clothes brush over his arms and legs. His brother-in-law, still not satisfied, reached for a battery powered vacuum, resembling a small, bright yellow hand dryer shaped like a pistol. He actually passed the machine over his bare torso and proceeded to vacuum his limbs. "Better job than the brush," Abe Tarnow said, "but I like to use both. To make sure nothing from the outside taints the waters. For your purification, Bartholomew," he laughed heartily.

The vacuum continued to buzz over his knees causing his towel to flutter. "You'll not be taking that into my *mikveh*," warned Tarnow, allowing his machine to pass surreptitiously under the towel.

His mikveh. This *mikveh* belongs to all the men of Datschlav, the same as the *mikveh* in the identical building next to the girls' school on *Rehov Sara* belongs to all the women. Tarnow is only the *mikveh* man, the superintendent of male immersers. Still, he acts like such a big shot. Like in the old days, when the village was first built. People never change, Baruch thought to himself.

Finally satisfied with the body check he had given Baruch, Tarnow sauntered over to the witness stand, a small podium, midway down the side of the pool. Stationing himself behind it, he adjusted the microphone resting on the top, handy for his instructions.

"Testing ... one, two, three ... Ready for your dive, Berkovitch?" he laughed uproariously. Baruch knew why. One couldn't dive into this *mikveh*. At the deep end it was only five feet and the bottom was slippery with silt. The microphone screeched as Tarnow continued laughing into it.

Tarnow's comments flowed endlessly. "How about a front crawl? I'm sure you are a fine swimmer, my friend, the best in Datschlav!" Again he knew only too well that none of the Datschlavers knew how to swim. He approached the ladder. On his stomach, hanging on to the bottom rung, he kicked his feet in protest. The brackish water splashed about him. Tarnow immediately yelled: "No splashing in the *mikveh*! No splashing in the *mikveh*!"

Baruch quickly climbed the ladder, grabbing his towel. Without acknowledging Tarnow, he made his way to one of the shower and rest rooms adjacent to the pool area. He closed the door behind him.

In the shower he adjusted the water as hot as he could

tolerate, letting it run down his body for fifteen minutes. Tarnow shouted at him from the other side of the door. "Leave some hot water for the next person. And remember, the funeral is at three. It's only one-thirty now. I'll be back in half an hour."

Baruch heard a loud buzz, followed by Tarnow's shrill voice. "My timer, up on the wall. I control it from my pocket bell boy. Have a good rest, my friend."

Baruch got out of the shower, carefully dried himself, and wrapped a thin, worn towel around his waist. "Can't they even buy decent towels?" he grumbled. He lay down on a cot pushed to one side of the cubicle and pulled the moth-eaten blanket over his shivering body. "And blankets? Can't they buy decent blankets? Or, what about heating the place? It's October . . . can't they turn the heat on?"

He looked around. A jail. That's what it is. A cell with a shower, a small sink, and a formica table crowded with brushes, combs, nail files, scissors, razors, cotton balls, creams, and soaps.

But the pale, green and pink ceramic tile floors, some tiles missing and dirt pushing up through the cracks reminded him of somewhere else. A room in an institution, one that had long since closed its doors to public inspection. A spider moved busily on the floor by the pedestal of the wash basin. Baruch's head pounded.

He could smell the heavy *mikveh* waters even through the closed door. Did he also smell the kill from the slaughter-house? No. The windows were sealed and the abbatoir was a good distance from the men's bathhouse. He dozed, fitfully dreaming.

Richard Vincennes stood beside his father, on the kill floor. Richard was wearing a pink florescent swim suit, a black silk cape, and matching top hat. The bathing suit had a silver belt with a gold buckle. Judah Leib wore his slaughterer's rubber apron over his black, baggy pants

and white cotton shirt, the sleeves rolled up at the el-
bows. He wore a white satin skull cap and he brandished
a slaughterer's knife, one with an exceedingly large, rec-
tangular blade. Brilliant light shone from the blade as
well as from Vincennes' gold belt buckle.

Baruch was awakened by Tarnow's high pitched voice from
the other side of the cubicle door. "You are up, Berkovitch?"

In the rebbe's study next to the synagogue, the Berkovitch
family waited. Faigele with her two children and his three
other sisters with their husbands and children. All together,
there were twenty-six relatives gathered to meet the rebellious son. The rebbe waited with them. When Tarnow and
Baruch walked into the study, the entire family rose. Then the
rebbe formally praised the son of the slaughterer, Judah Leib:
"I welcome you back to Datschlav, my boy. I give you and
your art my blessing."

Rebeccah Leah nearly fainted when she heard his pro-
nouncement, yet she weakly extended her arms to embrace
her son.

Fiona missed Bartholomew at the opening of her Montreal
retrospective. He had phoned from Datschlav to tell her the
unexpected news of his father's death, and she had of course
agreed that he should prolong his visit, offering to travel to
Datschlav to join him. When he had called, she hesitated to
display her enthusiasm about the success of her show, but
when Baruch kept asking, she succumbed, describing the
opening as a turning point in her career. She was pleased,

deliriously so, yet she was sorry and upset about Judah Leib. In a few days she would join Baruch, whether or not his people approved of their relationship.

After speaking to Baruch, she admitted to herself that a lot of the credit for her favourable reception should go to Danny Wintrob, a friend since childhood who had earned his own place of prominence in the art world as *Huit Heure*'s curator. Danny had a routine for publicising his artists. His guest list numbered close to one thousand and the invitations drew an enormous crowd to the gallery for her opening night. Within a few hours she had actually sold four of her sculptures and thirteen of her watercolours. Seventeen works in all. A record sale for any opening ever held at *Huit Heure*.

Wintrob's exuberance continued the next morning when he read aloud to her a review from *The Gazette*. Pierre Gaudois, a reputed curmudgeon among art critics, praised Fiona highly: "The gentleness of Shield's brushstroke contrasts markedly with her sculpting technique. It's as if her hands were as rigid as her medium. There are no soft contours, no easy positions. Shield's bronzes stand in stiff contortion, they have no movement; her watercolours, however, are in constant motion, their disposition totally feminine."

She told Danny that Gaudois sounded like another chauvenist critic, but he said it was a good review, the kind that arouses curiosity, bringing people into the gallery. He handed her the article and urged her to read on. She did, reluctantly. "Shields has a dual muse, the male for her sculpture, the female for her watercolours. She is a bi-gendered genius."

"Bullshit," she said to Danny, who snatched the paper back from her. Earlier that morning he had clipped the review, including a dramatic photograph of her with long, black hair falling abundantly on to her shoulders. Now, Danny pinned the clipping to a piece of black velvet, mounting it on an easel which he put in the gallery window. He directed a spotlight on to the article. The easle stood next to one of Fiona's sculptures, a six-foot male nude, his hair plastered artificially down the sides of his face, his wide eyes vacant beneath his bushy eyebrows, so bushy there was no separation between them. In his hands he held two braids the same length as his stiffly plastered hair. A plaque between his feet read: *Renegade Son*. Many of the gallery's clients had commented on the statue's hands which appeared flexible against a tense and unwavering bronze body. Only the hands had freedom.

Fiona left Montreal one week after her successful exhibition opening. She took the Métro to the Henri Bourassa station and then crossed the road to the bus terminal where she bought a ticket for Claremont-Ste Justine. She was given a choice of two tickets, one to take her to a shopping centre between the twin towns, and the other to take her five miles beyond Claremont's city limits. She took the second ticket and then walked to Gate 11 where both buses departed from every two hours.

On the bus Fiona took the novel she was currently reading out of her purse. She had read *St. Urbain's Horseman* when it first came out several years ago, but now that she was in Montreal again and her parents were in Israel, she was in the mood to remind herself of the insularity of the Main that Mordecai Richler depicted so perfectly, the secular equivalent to the Datschlavers' community.

Fiona thought about the Datschlavers when they lived on Jeanne Mance. She had tried to make friends with Hannah, Bartholomew's youngest sister. The Datschlaver girls' schoolyard was adjacent to the Shields family's long, narrow, back garden. Fiona's mother and father felt fortunate to have a place for her to play, since their property was at the corner of Jeanne Mance and Fairmount.

One day, Fiona's Indian rubber ball got stuck in a hole in the pine planked fence separating the two yards. Usually the fence, badly in need of repair, had several holes plugged with large wads of steel wool and pieces of newspaper. Her ball had knocked out the makeshift mending, and she was surprised to find a pudgy Datschlaver's face peeking back at her. She stared at the girl for a few minutes before mustering the courage to speak to her. Hannah didn't answer, and Fiona thought the child probably didn't understand or speak English, so she asked her a second time in Yiddish. Still no answer, and this time Hannah appeared frightened. The next day, however, when Fiona came to play in her back garden, she found her ball with a note taped to it.

Please, I cannot talk to you but I would like to watch you play in your garden. Sometimes I can write to you. I'll leave my letters in the hole in the fence where I first saw you. But I must be careful because I'm not allowed to communicate with *ordinary* Jewish children.

Your neighbour,

Hannah,
the youngest daughter of the slaughterer, Judah Leib
and the good Rebeccah Leah.

Indeed, Fiona, raised orthodox, was upset by her Hasidic neighbour, taught to shun her fellow Jew. Fiona learned then how strict the Datschlavers were, offering their children no freedom in matters such as friendship.

Fiona didn't see Hannah's face through the hole in the wood fence for the entire fall after she received the note. Not until winter, when she built a snow fort in her backyard, did she feel a pair of eyes watching her. For the three days Fiona spent building her fort bigger and bigger, Hannah's eyes watched, and on the third day, a snowball with a note inside it was pushed through the hole in the fence just as the bell rang at four-thirty in the afternoon ending the Datschlaver girls' recess. Datschlaver girls stayed in school until six o'clock, whereas Fiona was dismissed at three-thirty. Fiona read the note:

Communication between Hannah, a truly pious and devoted Datschlaver, daughter of the slaughterer, Judah Leib, and the good Rebeccah Leah, and the orthodox Jewess, Fiona Shields, daughter of Harry and Fanny Shields, is henceforth forbidden.

Cordially,

Rebbetzin Kasarkofski,
in the name of Mendel Yehudah, Grand Rebbe
of the Montreal Datschlavers.

The note bore the rebbe's official seal, three mountains, and the book, *Dinim*. Three rays of light pierced the Datschlaver commentary. The note, itself, was sealed with soft, red wax.

The bus stopped in Claremont. Two kerchiefed, pregnant women, wearing black, long-sleeved dresses boarded. As soon as they sat down they took out small leatherbound volumes from their handbags and began moving their lips silently. A few miles on the highway, just beyond the Texaco service station, the bus turned on to a dirt road. Fiona read the sign outside her window: *To Rehov Zion, La Manse Vincennes, L'Abbatoir Datschlav.* She had arrived.

"Hurry up, Hannah; Hurry, Sara, you are late," a voice called out when the bus opened its door for the last stop of the journey in front of the first bungalow on *Rehov Zion*. "It's four o'clock," the man said. "The store closes in fifteen minutes. If you need something, you better hurry." The black frocked Datschlaver took off towards a building with a huge sign in transliterated Yiddish reading *General Store*.

"The store," said Sara. "Does he think I can go to the store now? Doesn't he know I have to be home for my daughters?"

"And my children too," Hannah heartily agreed, even though only one of her daughters was old enough to go to school. Rachel gets home by four," she continued, "then I have to feed the babies."

"Always that Eliezar, he is trying to make a sale," Sara declared.

"Of course," said Hannah, "but I made my supper for tonight yesterday."

"I made ours then, too," Sara echoed her sister.

"Does he think we would go to see our doctor in Montreal without preparing our family's supper in advance? I made three pot roasts and four carrot puddings. Michele is peeling three dozen potatoes right now. I told her to soak them in ice water, then to dry them on paper towels, before she puts them in an oiled pan in the oven."

Fiona couldn't believe what she was hearing. Oblivious to their domestic work load, they chatted proudly until Hannah's voice changed considerably. "I think I did too much yesterday. On my feet in the kitchen from morning until night. I told the doctor about my varicose veins. But who wants to complain," she said, trying to maintain her usual level of spunkiness.

"Excuse me," Fiona interrupted, "aren't you Hannah Berkovitch?"

Hannah blushed when she heard her maiden name.

"Come," she said to her sister, "we'll be late!"

"Don't you remember me?" Fiona said. "From Jeanne Mance. My parents owned the store at the corner of Jeanne Mance and Fairmount, next to the Datschlaver girls' school. I was a friend of yours for a short time. You used to watch me through a hole in the fence separating your schoolyard from our garden."

Hannah smiled awkwardly and Fiona saw that the young woman's teeth were yellow and decayed.

"You're coming to Datschlav to see our family, aren't you?" Hannah asked.

"Yes," replied Fiona, "But I'm especially delighted to see you, Hannah, first, before the others."

"It's not good for a woman to be first." She looked down at her tremendous belly blooming under her breasts.

"You are pregnant," said Fiona. "Congratulations."

"No," said Hannah. "My stomach is swollen because of my hernia. I saw the doctor today, even though it is the *shiva* for my father, Judah Leib, *olav-ha-shalom*. Next week the doctors will operate. I don't want an operation but the doctor says I must have one if I want to have more children." A big smile lit up Hannah's face. "So, I'll have the operation . . . I must hurry home," she said, changing the subject.

"I understand," Fiona replied. "I must see the rebbe and Bartholomew." She corrected herself, "I mean Baruch, the son of Judah Leib, the slaughterer, *olav-ha-shalom*."

"*Olav-ha-shalom*," repeated Hannah, keeping her eyes downcast. "My brother, he is content? Is he at peace with *Ribonu shel Olam*?"

"He is no longer observant in the same way as the Datschlavers, if that's what you are referring to. He has a secular approach to Judaism."

"Secular? What is secular?"

"He thinks a lot about Judaism. He reads Jewish history and literature. You may not believe me, Hannah, but your brother is considered by many of our friends to be a very observant Jew. Both our Jewish and Gentile friends think of him as having a profound Jewish conscience. His work has been critically praised for its Jewish content."

"We know," said Hannah. "The rebbe told us this week that we are now permitted to be proud of Baruch's artistic achievements."

Fiona raised her eyes in astonishment. "Rebbe Mendel Yehudah publicly approved of your brother's paintings? Indeed this is precedent in the community?"

"Not the first," said Hannah.

"What do you mean?"

"I mean, Faigele, my eldest sister. She, too, is precedent."

"Over and over," sighed Sara. "Ah, Judah Leib, *olav-ha-shalom*, thank *Ribonu shel Olam*, you are free now."

"Free," sang Hannah. "May you enter *The World to Come*.

You were a good father."

"Amen," said Sara.

"Amen," repeated Fiona, fearing her silence might break the spell.

"You shall see for yourself, Fiona Shields, what has happened to our Faigele. But now you must come to my house. Have a cup of tea before you go to the rebbe's. I'll call the rebbetzin and tell her you are here," Hannah continued. "You can rest, have something to eat."

"Yes," answered Fiona, "whatever you think best."

7

Fiona followed Hannah and Sara from the bus stop at the end of the dirt road and Square *Rehov Zion*. They walked past *Rehov Moshe* and *Rehov Yehoshua*, the girls' school and the women's ritualarium at the corner of *Rehov Sara* next to Hannah and Peretz's house.

"Come in Sara," Hannah invited her sister. "I want to give you half a pan of *parve* ice cream. You can sit for a few minutes and have a cup of tea with our visitor, too."

"I'd love to Hannah, but I promised Mama I'd drop by to see if she needs help. You know how many come for *davening*," Sara said, parking herself on the doorstep while Hannah wiped her feet on the worn rug in the front hall. Rachel, Hannah's nine-year-old daughter, rushed from the kitchen to the vestibule to welcome her mother. She stared at Fiona's dress which reached only to her knees and at her nylons which were the same colour as her bare skin. A long-sleeved jacket and a head scarf, thank *Ribonu shel Olam*, but still those exposed legs. Who was she, this she-demon, Rachel wondered.

"Fiona is an old friend," Hannah told her daughter.

"When I met your mother," Fiona told Rachel, "I was just about your age."

"Oh, Mama," exclaimed Rachel, "where did you find her?"

"Back in Montreal, dear, before we moved to Datschlav. Fiona lived next door to the girls' school." Hannah presented her sister with half a pan of *parve* ice cream. Fiona could hardly believe her eyes. Half the pan looked like enough to serve thirty people.

Sara thanked her sister and told her she would see her later. Hannah returned to the dining room where Fiona was waiting. She introduced her daughter. "Fiona is related to someone to whom we are also related."

"I knew it! I knew it!" cried Rachel. "I could tell right away. She is the wife of Uncle Baruch!"

"Yes . . . " said Hannah. "But Uncle Baruch and Fiona have no children." Hannah felt she had to explain since the child would want to know where Fiona's children were.

Fiona tried to help Hannah. "Until now, I haven't even told Baruch the good news as I found out only this morning, before I left Montreal. Baruch and I are expecting. We always wanted one child but we waited and planned for a long time."

"One child? But you must have at least two. A boy and a girl," said Rachel, sounding older than her years, like a well-rehearsed mother-to-be. Fiona was her mother's age and was having her first child, a planned pregnancy, while her mother had eleven children and had not planned any of them.

Fiona tried to explain. "Back in Montreal, life is different . . . "

"*Shaah*, enough talk," Hannah insisted, "let's have our tea. And some yeast buns. I made them this morning before I went to the doctor. With cheese for flavour. I make my own cheddar," she proudly added. "My own butter, too. We'll have some strawberry jam. A little sugar at this time of day is important when you're expecting. You must consider the child," Hannah explained as she stared at Fiona's sheer stockings, thanking aloud the Master of the Universe that her black nylons concealed varicose veins resulting from eleven pregnancies, enlarged and swollen from standing long hours in the kitchen.

Hannah scooped two teaspoons of jam onto Fiona's plate, saying, "Eat and enjoy! I'll call the rebbetzin so that she can tell the rebbe that you have arrived. Rachel, dear, bring me the phone. I'll sit down. Put my feet up for a few minutes on this footstool. Ah, that's better." She settled herself with some difficulty, adjusting her long, black dress, making sure it hung properly down to her ankles. Satisfied, she began stroking her swollen stomach.

The phone cord was long enough for Hannah to shuffle about the dining room and kitchen. She certainly couldn't afford to be idle when she talked on the phone. It rang endlessly from morning to night.

Rachel wound the interminable cord into small coils, arranging them neatly under her mother's chair. The phone rang just as she was about to dial the rebbetzin's number. "Eat! Eat!" she called back to Fiona before she answered. "Hello, Rebbetzin, what a coincidence, I was just going to call you. The doctor, yes, of course, bad news, always bad news ... never mind, I'll tell you later ... Now, I have a visitor from Montreal ... Baruch has told you about her ... Fiona Shields."

"I thought you were married to Uncle Baruch?" Rachel asked. "How come you call yourself Shields?"

Fiona, about to explain, was silenced by Hannah. She excused herself from her conversation with the rebbetzin, asking her daughter to help out in the kitchen. To make sure Rachel would be kept occupied Hannah instructed, "Slice a dozen tomatoes and peel four pounds of carrots. When you're finished, put the vegetables in the refrigerator. And don't forget to clean up. Go on now."

Hannah continued talking with the rebbetzin. "Yes, I think she should see the rebbe first ... yes, I heard, everyone is talking about how long the rebbe spoke with Baruch ... yes, I agree, he may also want to speak with Fiona Shields for a long time . . . especially under the circumstances. Rebbetzin, should I give her a pair of black stockings? She's wearing sheer nylons . . . okay . . . and Rebbetzin, don't worry, she's wearing a head scarf . . . I'll send her over in half an hour." Hannah hung up. The phone immediately rang again.

"Hello, Mother? The doctor? What should a doctor say? Always bad news . . . that's why I go so seldom . . . but never mind, I have a guest . . . from Montreal . . . I can't talk now . . . I'll be over after supper. We'll make a vegetable soup with *flanken* and lots of marrow bones. A good, thick soup. Goodbye, Mama."

Hannah hung up, looking anxiously at Fiona. Nervously, she called to her daughter in the kitchen, "Rachel, better cut up some celery. Three bunches."

Hannah turned to Fiona, "Everything is for the children," she grinned, displaying her neglected teeth while her childish eyes sparkled. "And for the men. Everything is for them, too."

Hannah stared at Fiona's legs. "Maybe for the sake of the men and the rebbe, and most important for *Ribonu shel Olam*, you'll put on black stockings. As a sign of respect," she hastened to add.

"I certainly will not," Fiona replied. "I don't think my stockings are of concern to The Holy One."

Hannah continued, "Fiona, I don't understand how you can do this?"

"Do what?" Fiona intoned angrily.

"Come here. Dressed like that," said Hannah, fixing her eyes on Fiona's flesh-toned knees. She would have said more, but just then her husband, Peretz, marched into the room with their seven sons, the three eldest boys, Yehudah, Reuben, and Yosef, immersed in their spiritual readings. Only when they saw their mother chatting with a stranger did they close their books, placing them on the shelf by the dining room entrance. Beside the bookshelf was a sink. Father and sons washed their hands, drying them carefully, repeating a blessing. They took their places in a row opposite Fiona at the dining room table divided by a thin olive wood partition through its centre, signifying the separation between men and women.

"Tea, Peretz, before *mincha*," asked Hannah.

"Some tea before *mincha*," repeated Peretz and his boys in chorus. Fiona felt like she was sitting in a synagogue.

"Rachel, get some tea for your Papa," said Hannah premonitorily. "Some hot chocolate for your brothers. Use the two percent milk with carob powder," she instructed Rachel. "No whipping cream. A dash of cinnamon would be nice too. And some *mandlebroit* and cheese buns. No jam." Her orders seemed endless.

Peretz and his older sons sat with their heads bowed, silent and preoccupied. The younger boys suppressed giggles, sneaking a glance at the strange female in their presence.

"And who is this woman?" Peretz asked, without lifting his eyes.

"Rachel," said Hannah, "come here, and sit beside me."

"O thank you," said the child, who had been waiting nervously at the kitchen door for an invitation.

Fiona was surprised that Peretz noticed her. Indeed, he seemed in another realm.

"Fiona Shields," she dared to answer Hannah's husband. "Baruch's wife." How could she tell these pious men that she was not married to Baruch. Immediately, she added, "We're expecting our first child." Still, she could not resist adding, "We've waited because we wanted to establish our careers first."

"What's this, *our* careers? A woman must have children. Even Rachel who is only nine knows this, don't you, my dear?"

"Oh, yes, Papa, when you and Rebbe arrange my marriage, *Ribonu shel Olam* willing, I shall be just like Mama, with many, many children. Maybe more than Mama," she said eagerly.

Fiona excused herself to go to the bathroom. Why was she

being so hard on the Datschlavers, she kept asking herself until she opened the bathroom door and the odour overwhelmed her. Too many people used one toilet and the plumbing was obviously inadequate. Yet, the facility was modern, its floor and walls pink tiled. In the doorless vanity underneath the sink sat a pile of small, white linen squares, freshly laundered with a note nearby reading, *for bedikah*. Fiona saw a spot of blood near the base of the toilet. She had always felt repelled by the *bedikah* custom. Yet she forced herself to read the instructions printed on a card next to the clean, white cloths.

It is advisable for the examination to put one leg on a small footstool (or its equivalent) while in a standing position, and to insert the soft, white cloth which has been wrapped around your finger into your body as far as possible. You must move the cloth to and fro, into every fold and crevice, as far as the finger can penetrate. (It is preferable that you take the cloth out, examine it, and insert another cloth). This cloth, if possible, should remain there until night. If you find it difficult to tolerate for so long, you may take it out and examine it thoroughly. If it is not perfectly white, whatever the colour may be, a competent *dayan* must be consulted. If the cloth is perfectly white, you may begin counting the clean days. In the aforementioned case, where the cloth did not remain internally until night, it is desireable that about fifteen minutes before the appearance of the stars, you should insert a soft, clean cloth, and keep it there until the stars appear. The cloth that is removed should be examined thoroughly and carefully put away in a clean place until the next morning when it should be reexamined by daylight.

She had read enough. The thought of a Datschlaver woman, swabbing herself to determine her state of cleanliness, and yet not able to make the ultimate decision concerning her purity disgusted her. If there was the smallest stain, the woman had to send the cloth via the female witness, who in Datschlav was Hannah, to the *dayan*, the male judge. Peretz, Hannah's husband, the man she had just met, was the sole arbiter. He alone vouchsafed the collective Datschlaver pudenda, consulting the rebbe in particularly dubious situations, never consulting the women themselves.

She put the card back, then tried to open the window but it was sealed. However, there was a fan in the ceiling. She switched it on. Slowly the air circulated. She felt weak from the combination of bathroom odours. She heard a knock. "Are you all right?" Rachel asked. "Yes," she replied weakly. But when she opened the door she collapsed into the young girl's arms.

She woke up in Rachel's room. The child had pressed a cool cloth to her forehead. "What happened to me?" Fiona asked.

"You fainted," Rachel answered. "You must be tired from your trip and you're expecting."

She sounded so concerned, so sweet. Why did she think that the child and her mother were not content? She was wrong to judge them.

"Is Fiona okay?" Hannah asked from the doorway.

"Yes, Mama."

"Are you okay?" Hannah asked Fiona directly.

Fiona nodded.

"I'm so relieved," she said. "It is probably difficult for you to confront our life when you're not a part of it. But let me assure you, Fiona Shields, we Datschlavers have established a Davidic kingdom in Quebec. Remember this." She turned and left the room. Fiona stared at Rachel's beautiful black braids while Hannah's words rang in her ears. "Can you get me a pair of black stockings?" she asked the child. "I'll put them on before I go to see the rebbe."

"Fiona Shields has passed out," Hannah announced. "She's resting now in the girls' bedroom."

"Resting is she?" replied Hannah's husband condescendingly.inglyinglyingly "The sooner she leaves, the better. She's a bad influence on Rachel. Fortunately our other daughters are too young to take notice."

He signalled his sons to get up from the table, the young ones to go off to their rooms to begin their homework, the older boys to accompany him to the men's *mikveh*. In *Dinim*, Rebbe Shlomo Yitzchak, the founding Datschlaver rebbe, decreed daily immersion for all male adults, including boys who had celebrated their thirteenth birthdays. "To the *mikveh*, fellas. Take your books along. We'll have time to study before and after our immersion. Hannah, we'll be home at seven-thirty. Please see that supper is ready because tonight we have a *Dinim* lesson from eight to eleven." Peretz took four cheese buns and a hunk of Hannah's homemade cheddar as he got up from the table. Peretz wanted to take all the books off the shelf, lest the Shields woman contaminate them by her presence. He had a good mind to stop by the rebbe's on his way to the men's ritualarium to tell him how distasteful he found her. But for several years now, Peretz had moved further and further from the rebbe's favour. Richard Vincennes and Faigele took all his time. Peretz kissed his prayerbook and tucked it into the folds of his gaberdine before saying to Hannah, "See you at seven-thirty, *Yirtzeh HaShem*.

"*Yirtzeh HaShem*," Hannah repeated, her eyes downcast.

Fiona returned to the dining room supported by Rachel, just after Peretz and his sons left.

"You're wearing black stockings. How wonderful," said Hannah. She checked the time. "*Ribonu shel Olam*, you're late for the rebbe. I better phone Rebbetzin. Rachel, show Fiona the way to the rebbe's. When you get back, set the table for supper."

The phone rang, but before she answered it she took the time to curtsy to Fiona. "Now, you look perfect. Go to the rebbe's," she smiled, exposing her bad teeth.

"You don't go very often to the dentist, do you?" Fiona asked.

"Everything I do is for the children. And for the men. I don't have time to go to the dentist." Plunking herself down, she picked up the phone. "Rebbetzin," she answered enthusiastically, "I was just about to call you. They're on their way. Rachel and Fiona. She's a pin of a thing. And doesn't eat, even though she's expecting. No wonder she fainted!"

They walked over to the rebbe's, Rachel providing a running commentary. "This is Aunt Bryna's house," the girl declared as they passed the bungalow next to her family's. "Aunt Bryna and Uncle Shmuel are responsible for gardening, snow shovelling, and garbage collection." She pointed to their side driveway. "At the end is the garbage eating machine. Such a noise it makes . . . var-oom, var-oom," said Rachel with a sparkle in her eyes. "Uncle Shmuel makes rounds twice a week with his truck. That one," she pointed to the blue van parked in the street, *Garbage* painted in transliterated Yiddish on the side. "What the machine won't eat, Uncle Shmuel drives to Claremont."

They crossed *Rehov Datschlav* approaching the synagogue. "I think I'll pop in and have a look around," Fiona said, as they arrived at the front door. Rachel told Fiona she couldn't use the front entrance. "You must use the women's entrance on the side of the building facing the rebbe's house," the child explained.

"Don't be ridiculous," Fiona replied. "This is 1980. I can go in the front door if I choose to."

"But it's a *shul*," Rachel said.

"Yes, a house of worship," said Fiona. "Exactly the reason why I should enter by whichever entrance I choose."

"But women aren't allowed to enter by the front door," the girl repeated. "If someone sees you, you will be punished."

"Don't be foolish, Rachel. You wait here."

The dimly lit hallway was large and wide. Prayer shawls flowed out of cubbyholes and dirty ash trays rested on chairs lined up against the walls. Garbage cans filled with discarded food and its wrappings cluttered the foyer, the windows of which were covered by black, drawn curtains.

Fiona passed through quickly to the main hall. By contrast, it was brightly lit, and she immediately realized that this synagogue was similar to many of the small *shtiebels* she had frequented as a child. Basically a large study room with tables and benches, the Holy Ark tucked inconspicuously against the eastern wall. A back hall led to a second room for the women. Two old men sat hunched over large volumes at the table in the centre of the room while three teenage boys rocked back and forth in their seats by the window as they studied. By the synagogue entrance, a man slept, snoring loudly. Fiona recognized him, Rachel's father. His chest moved rapturously up and down, knocking one of Hannah's cheese buns out of one of his unbuttoned bulging suit jacket pockets.

The old men paid no attention to Fiona, but the teenagers, Rachel's three brothers, stared up from their books. Fiona asked if she could speak to the beadle, but Yosef, whom she had addressed, declared angrily, "Women aren't allowed in this section of the synagogue."

His brother, Moshe, spoke, "How did you get in here?"

"Through the front door, naturally. Rachel, your sister brought me here. She's waiting outside."

"Didn't she tell you not to use the front entrance?" asked the third boy, Yehudah.

"She told me to go to the side of the building, to the women's synagogue."

"So, why didn't you?"

"Because I wanted to see the men's *shul*."

"This is a *shul*, not a museum," snapped Yosef.

"Besides, it made sense to come here. I have an appointment with the rebbe."

This time, one of the old men spoke up. "You won't find the rebbe here at this time of day. He's next door in his house."

The other old man said, "I think you meant to say you have an appointment with the rebbetzin."

"No, with the rebbe," Fiona replied firmly.

"With rebbe, she has an appointment?" he muttered sardonically.

"What are you studying?" Fiona asked.

"I'll tell you," he said, clearing his nose and throat at the same time, the phlegm issuing forth landing on Fiona's right foot. "Get out of here," he coughed. "By the correct door," he pointed to the dark back hallway leading to the women's synagogue. Rachel's brothers laughed. The old men instructed them to take their places at the long study table. "Open your *Dinim*," said one of them in an uncompromising voice. "Yosef," he continued, "you are only on page one hundred and twenty. You started on page one hundred and eighteen this morning. Only two *blatt*, today? Five *blatt*, you must do!" He sneered as he looked over at Fiona, wiping the spittle off her shoe.

"Forget this creature, all of you. She has no business being here."

Fiona fled to the women's sanctuary. "I'll report you to Rebbe Kasarkofski, you she-demon!" The old man roared.

"Finish your *blatt*," he said sternly to the teenage boys.

In the dark hallway deliberately kept that way by a twenty-five watt bulb in the one and only ceiling fixture, Fiona found a long, narrow mirror which gave off only the slightest reflection. Shelves on either side of this mirror were filled with stray articles of outer clothing, the odd book and several empty pill bottles, all labelled: "Mrs. Pattenick, the good Malka; Mrs. Levy, the good Judith." Piles of clean rags were piled in one corner. Fiona reached for one to shine her right pump which the old man had covered with spittle.

Her head scarf and her black stockings, even her long-sleeved dress, as evidenced by the mirror's dim likeness, were obviously not enough concealment for the Datschlaver men. "Damn them, anyway," she muttered, pulling off her scarf. She combed her hair into a loose chignon with several extravagant curls bobbing at her ears. Her fingers moved adeptly. She was good with her hair. Excited, she thought about Bartholomew who loved to stroke it.

Fiona folded the flower-printed scarf into a narrow band, wrapping it around her chignon, letting the end of the scarf fall over her shoulder, as her hair would have fallen had it been brushed to one side.

She avoided the women's sanctuary, leaving by the women's entrance. Rachel waited on the steps outside. She screamed when she saw Fiona.

"You have hair," she exclaimed, slowly taking her hands from her eyes. "You must not let anyone see you. Quick, your scarf."

"Why?" said Fiona. "My hair is for your Uncle Baruch's enjoyment."

"The rebbetzin won't let you see the rebbe."

"What does my hair have to do with the rebbe?"

"It's a *din*," Rachel replied, panicking.

"Rachel, you have beautiful, thick, black hair. When you go to the *mikveh* for the first time, before you marry, you will have to cut your hair. You will have to shave your scalp, not just once, but every month, God forbid. Do you realize what your rebbe asks of you?"

Rachel stared at her black oxfords. "It's a *din*. A *din* is a law."

"Are you happy with the *din*, Rachel?" Fiona asked.

"You perform a *din*. You do not question. After you are happy."

"Ah, that's it! After! But what about *before*? Look at your beautiful braids. Warm in winter. Soft to touch for your beloved to whom you will be married . . . "

"My father is right!" the girl screamed. "You are a she-demon!"

"Did your father tell you not to listen to me?"

"Mama, too. They told me to close my ears to what you say."

"Is that what you want to do?"

"Yes," the girl answered, staring icily at Fiona.

At the Grande Rebbe Mendel Yehudah's house, the children pressed their noses against the living room window. They began jumping up and down when they saw Fiona and Rachel. A stranger visiting Datschlav was always an exciting and welcome event, providing diversion from an otherwise regimented and austere life. Sometimes the stranger brought gifts from the secular world. One boy collected badges; another marbles; a third, hockey cards.

The mothers indulged their children, letting them have their collections. Only a few of the fathers knew. They didn't approve; however, they agreed that mothers knew best about a child's games.

The jubilance of the children caused their mothers, Frima,

Shaindel, Rifkeh, and Rachel, the rebbe's four daughters, to run from the kitchen, hustling their daughters and sons to separate tables for supper.

"Can we ask for presents from Montreal?" asked Shmuel, one of the rebbe's grandsons.

"Wait, Shmuel, we'll see what the rebbetzin says," his mother, Frima answered.

"Sometimes, Grandma doesn't let me ask for presents. You must ask, Mama."

"And you must eat so you can begin your homework like a good boy," said Frima, tousling her son's sidelocks, hesitating a moment to enjoy their warm softness. He's only a child, she thought to herself. I'll ask the stranger myself, she decided, as her mother, the dowager, strode into the room.

Marching directly to the window she pushed aside the sheer curtains. Catching her first glimpse of Fiona Shields, the rebbetzin shook her head. *Ribonu shel Olam,* she said, "what will I do? The girl has no modesty." She hurried to the hall cupboard, liberating her biggest head scarf. Like everyone in Datschlav, she assumed that Fiona and Baruch were married. Rebbetzin did not wait for Fiona or Rachel to knock. Scarf in hand, she opened the front door. "Welcome to Datschlav, wife of our beloved Baruch, son of Judah Leib, *olav-ha-shalom.*" Twisting the scarf, she said, "Come in, come in. I'm happy to see you, my dear . . . You see, girls," Rebbetzin continued, "she knows to wear black stockings."

"She knows," the girls echoed.

"But, my dear," said the rebbetzin, changing her tone, "if you wish to see the rebbe, please cover your head."

"Must I?"

"Yes, please. Why cause trouble?"

"Trouble," Rebbetzin's daughters sang.

"I'm sorry, I won't wear a head scarf."

Disquieted the rebbetzin tried a different approach. "I'd like to show you something." Opening the top drawer of the hall console she began rummaging through a pile of photographs, selecting one of a woman without a head scarf walking away from the home of the rebbe. The woman's hair appeared bloodstained.

"You wouldn't want such a thing to happen to you?" asked the rebbetzin. "I'm telling you for your own good, the men lose control of themselves when they see a married woman with hair. They will throw stones at your abomination. Please, my child, wear this headscarf," urged the rebbetzin, handing it to her.

"But my hair is pinned up," said Fiona, protesting. "Besides," she complained, "why does my hair concern them?"

"It's a *din*," droned the daughters.

Fiona pushed the scarf back into Rebbetzin's hands. "I'll take my chances."

"Your decision is final?" asked the rebbetzin.

"Final," said Fiona.

"Final!" sang the horrified girls.

"Please come into the living room and sit down. I'll tell the rebbe that you are here. He is having a meeting, before *mincha*. Your Baruch is with him. So is his sister, Faigele." Rebbetzin crossed the room to Rebbe's office. She slipped inside, closing the door behind her.

Fiona watched the children and their mothers while she waited. Rebbetzin and Rebbe's daughters came out of the kitchen carrying four white enamel basins filled with water for the children to wash their hands. Next they brought in large pitchers of apple juice and bowls of ice. The meal consisted of several platters of sliced brisket, cabbage rolls, and carrot pudding, as well as bowls of salad and kasha. Fiona could not believe the quantities of food dispensed. In between mouthfuls, Shmuel smirked at Fiona, "Don't worry," he said, "you'll get some food after we men eat."

"I'm not the least bit concerned," she said drily. "Besides, I'm not hungry."

Rebbetzin returned from Rebbe's office. She had left the door ajar and Fiona could see Baruch standing beside the rebbe.

Rebbetzin formally announced, "The rebbe will see Fiona Shields."

In the kitchen tongues wagged, "Shields? She keeps her maiden name. Poor Judah Leib, *olav-ha-shalom*, it is good he is not here to see such shame. Terrible . . . terrible . . . "

"The Evil Eye shines on the family of the slaughterer," acknowledged one of the mothers before she passed a huge bowl of *parve* ice cream to the children. "Looks good," Fiona said to the passing woman.

"Chocolate and banana. I can get you the recipe. Enough for twenty four. You can cut the ingredients in half if you don't need that much."

"Can you really?" Fiona asked.

"Come by the kitchen after you see the rebbe. I'll introduce you to my sisters," she bravely added.

Fiona found herself touching her chignon and the sides of her hair, including the few loose curls, to make sure she looked just right for Baruch.

"Sit down, sit down," said the rebbe, waving her in. "How good to have you here. You look lovely, my dear, and your man, Baruch, tells me that you are doing well with your . . . *career*?"

"Baruch's exaggerating," said Fiona. "He's far more famous than I."

"The reviews of her show have been extraordinary. She's far too modest," Baruch boasted.

The rebbe grew silent. He fixed his eyes on Fiona's hair, especially the few loose curls. He got up and went over to her, sternly pulling the narrow scarf from her chignon. Fiona trembled as her hair fell, and Baruch appeared terrified.

The rebbe began gently stroking Fiona's hair. After what seemed an excruciatingly long silence, he spoke. "My Faigele here used to have such hair. I didn't want her to marry, her hair was so beautiful. Such pleasure it gave me. Remember Faigele," he said, while his wife and the others sat silently. "You know," he continued, "in Datschlav, we have many laws. One of them is *mikveh* and all the laws associated with the ritual immersion, not just from the Bible and the *Shulchan Aruch* but from *Dinim*, the laws of the first Datschlaver Rebbe, Shlomo Yitzchak. How can a woman be totally clean if her hair contaminates her?" he said softly as he continued to stroke Fiona's hair. "These follicles can hide all sorts of bacteria, dandruff, and yes, I will say it, lice. The witness, our Hannah, inspects the women before their immersions. You see, my child, the scalp must be shaved clean, except for the triangular tuft, for matching purposes on the Sabbath and other holidays and as a symbol . . . " Here, Rebbe made a victory sign with his index and third fingers.

"Oh, how I wish the Datschlavers did not have such a law. Faigele, here, knows the anguish it brings. For herself. For all our Datschlaver women."

Faigele suddenly felt emboldened, braver than she could ever remember feeling. She rose from her chair as she ripped her scarf from her head. Due for immersion at the *mikveh* in a few days, the stubble on her scalp appeared monstrously ugly. Rebbe held his hands to his face. "Please," he cried out, "I order you to put that scarf back on your head. I cannot bear to look at you."

"Excuse me, Rebbe," said Fiona passively, "this law of yours . . . must the women keep their head scarves on when they make love?"

The rebbe taken by surprise, still felt compelled to answer. "They can do what they want," he said, restraining his anger. "What does a man know when he's in bed with his wife. When he performs the act of love, it's always dark. The prescribed hours for sexual union are from four to six in the morning," he proclaimed with unwavering certainty. "Anyone who performs the act of love before or after these hours is doing so when heaven's gates are closed. Sexual union at nonprescribed hours may have disastrous consequences in our incorruptible world. Take heed."

"The world?" asked Fiona.

"Our fellow Datschlavers' world. Whether they live in New York, London, or Jerusalem, our brothers on occasion have reported earthquakes, hurricanes, and draught, the result of illicit sexual union when the gates of heaven are closed! Lilith performs these evils. The host of angels are not available to stop the she-demon as she roams the earth in search of lustful couplings in the non-prescribed hours. Now, once and for all, hide your shame," he screamed at Faigele. "You, Lilith, you!"

Part
TWO

1

Richard Vincennes looked up from his neatly arranged column of numbers. He had been studying since dinner, three hours earlier, so that the sight of both coffee and cognac beside his accounting book and the warmth of Sonia's hands kneading his shoulders were welcome until she quietly announced, "Richard, I'm going to have a baby."

"What are you talking about?" he asked, without turning around. He looked out the window above his desk. A perfect quarter moon. "I thought that diaphragm of yours was reliable."

"So did I, Richard. Believe me, so did I." She turned away, but he pulled her back on to his lap. She was shivering. Shivering, always a sign she was upset. Her pink angora sweater felt soft under his fingers. "I want you to have our baby," he told her, his hands resting on her already broadening hips, then back to her tummy, softened by her sweater, petting in slow, small circles, feeling with his fingertips for a trace of his child. "How many months?" he asked. He felt he was entitled to know.

"Three," she whimpered. "I can still have an abortion." Tear slipping out of her right eye. Always the right eye first.

He hated to see her cry. He got up, taking her with him. Tear coming out of the left eye now. Leading her to the sofa in front of the fireplace. Walking to the bar beside the bookcase. "Here, have a drink. It will make you feel better."

"Okay," she sobbed, taking a sip. "How can I have our child?" she said, refusing to look at him, wiping her tears with her handkerchief.

"You love me, don't you?"

"Of course, I love you."

"Then, why can't you have our child?"

She didn't answer. He walked back to his desk to stare out of the window of their third floor rooms into the night. The quarter moon laughing. He sipped the rest of his cognac. "I need some air," he told Sonia. "I think I'll go for a walk."

Sonia stood, her watery eyes clear enough to register panic. "Don't go, please. I can't be alone."

He took off his coat and put it on the sofa. Poured himself another cognac. "You want another?"

"No, thank you." At last, she spoke. "I've filled out an application for Boston University."

"You've been a busy little bee, haven't you?" He sat down beside her. "I suppose you made an appointment for an abortion, too."

"This Friday," she said, matter of factly.

"Is that what you really want?" he asked.

She moved closer. Again he felt the softness of her sweater. Soon she was clinging to him as he struggled with her jeans.

An hour later, she had fallen asleep in his arms. He got up quietly and left the apartment. Even though it was April, winter was having its final fling. The icy rain made his ears tingle. In two months he would receive his Bachelor of Arts degree from McGill. He had planned to spend the summer with his parents in Claremont-Ste Justine. It was to be his last summer with them for a long while. Since he had been at McGill, he had promised himself he would travel, but each spring when classes were over, he found himself back home again. In Boston, this would not be the case. Earlier that winter he had received his acceptance from Harvard Business School.

Sonia was already wheedling her way to Boston. She had planned to go to the University of Toronto, to the School of Social Work, but as soon as Richard received his Harvard acceptance, she began writing for calendars from at least a dozen schools in the Boston area.

They had been lovers for almost a year, having lived together since October. When they first met in a downtown Montreal bookshop, they had spoken because there was only one copy of the book they both wanted. "You take it," Richard had insisted. "I come here often. They regularly stock Emily Dickinson's poetry."

"Are you a student at McGill?" Richard asked.

"Yes, third year. Psychology."

"I'm finishing my third year, too," he volunteered. "Would you like to go for a beer?"

"Never drink beer. But a glass of wine might be a good idea," her velvet eyes suddenly looking like a scared squirrel's. She didn't know him, yet appeared to consider a glass of wine at a nearby café a harmless indulgence.

That was almost a year ago on a warm sunny day in early June. Now, the following April, Richard found himself walking down Hutchison towards Sherbrooke to the same café where he and Sonia had their first date. He took the same booth, near the back, ordered a double Remy Martin, and settled in, listening to the chanteuse. She reminded him of Sonia.

Sonia Mogell. Born in Warsaw in 1931. One year older than him, yet she seemed decades older. In 1943, she had left Warsaw, her parents taking her to Przewodowa, a small town with a monastery, convent, and hospital affiliated with the local church. The Abbot had promised safety for the Mogelonsky daughters, Sonia, age eleven, and Rose, thirteen. They worked in a hospital, folding bandages, scrubbing floors, bringing food for the sick and wounded.

The girls' diet was meager. Thin potato soup, scavenged potato peels, coarse bread, a variety of beans, some beets, and apples. Rose developed a stomach ailment, a constant state of bloat causing pressure on her colon. The condition grew worse. She had to limit her diet to watery soup and the occasional slice of dry bread. Sonia and Rose remained in Przewodowa until 1946, the sole survivors of the Mogelonsky family. The Abbot, aided by the British Jewish Congress, arranged for the girls to be adopted by a childless English couple, Sam and Ethyl Horowitz of Black Heath, close to London. Rose died of her stomach ailment within weeks of her arrival in England. Sonia was alone.

Sonia beside him now. Their first night together. When he made love to her, he realized how much she needed him. She still needed him, didn't she, he asked himself, but not enough to have his child. He made his decision, he would leave Sonia. He would go alone to Boston.

He paid for his cognac, leaving a generous tip. The waitress smiled, brushing the side of his arm with her long, red fingernails. "*Merci, Monsieur,*" she flirted. He left the café resolved to tell Sonia he did not want to live with her in Boston. She would shiver, she would cling. "You're all I have," she would say.

Richard pulled up the collar on his raincoat to protect himself from the cold drizzle. As he was about to cross Sherbrooke, he heard sirens. There had been an accident. A woman run over by a bus. Richard passed the covered body. "She's dead," said one female onlooker. "It was very messy! And she was so young. Only nineteen."

Suddenly Richard felt remorse for his earlier decision in the café. After the abortion, everything would return to normal. He and Sonia would grow closer. He changed his mind. He would not go to Boston without her.

He walked quickly now planning in his mind what Boston would be like, the two of them living together, Sonia studying at a small college, he, at Harvard Business School. Later, she would have his child, when she was more secure, after the memories of the war softened, after he helped her to forget.

Outside their rooming house on Hutchison an ambulance stood waiting. Some of the tenants had gathered. The fire department was also present. Richard's landlady, Madame Follette, rushed over. She put her hand on Richard's shoulder. "*Mon Dieu,*" she said, "*Je suis désolée. Elle est morte. Sa tête dans la four. Les fumes sont terrible . . . Mon Dieu.*"

2

Lou Greisman made three calls the morning after Sonia's suicide. The first was to Claude and Isabelle Vincennes and the second to Richard. He wanted them to meet him at the Ritz for lunch. The third call was to Mendel Yehudah Kasarkofski, the Datschlaver Rebbe.

"There's been an unexpected death," he told Mendel Yehudah. "One of the Congress orphans. We would like the Datschlavers to bury the girl." "We" meant "I." Lou Greisman was making this phone call on his own, not in his capacity as President of the Canadian Jewish Congress.

"Unexpected death?" queried Mendel Yehudah, his voice expressing genuine concern.

"A suicide," replied Greisman.

"Sorry, Mr. Greisman. We can't touch a suicide."

"But this is a special case. I thought you might bend the rules."

"Not the rules, Greisman. The Law. You are asking me to tamper with Datschlaver Law."

"Sonia Mogell was a courageous young woman. A martyr," Greisman cautiously added. "I thought the Datschlavers would be interested. I guess I was wrong."

"A martyr, you say? That could make a difference. If she is really a martyr, we might possibly proceed."

"You will consider her burial then? I knew you would."

"Come over right away. We'll discuss the details. Be here by ten."

When he arrived at the *shtiebel*, a bevy of young girls paraded up the front path, presided over by the rebbetzin, Mendel

71

Yehudah's wife. They came from the building next door. In their early teens, they still had long hair. Datschlaver daughters cut their hair as little as possible before they were married.

"Step aside, girls," ordered the rebbetzin when she saw Lou Greisman. The rebbetzin blew her whistle which she wore around her neck, the signal for her troop to curtsy.

Lou turned the handle on the bell below the window of the front door. The beadle asked routinely: "Who are you? What do you want?" After consulting his book he gestured to Lou to enter the dingy hallway. "First door on your right. The rebbe is expecting you."

The girls had followed Lou Griesman into the building, stationing themselves in the front room. Waiting for further instructions from their mistress, they hummed a melancholy tune, a song that Lou thought he was familiar with, the words of which were barely discernable.

Mendel Yehudah swayed to and fro in the far corner of his study, his voice chiming in with that of the girls in the front room. "Leave the door open," he instructed Lou, "and please come over and stand close to me." Facing the east wall, the Rebbe bowed deeply, before he turned to greet Lou. "You heard the girls in the front room? They are preparing Sonia Mogell's shroud."

At that moment, the singing grew louder, and Lou was able to make out the words:

In the clouds where you shall rest
where thou shalt be duly blessed
like the angels pure and white
we shall help thee soar tonight
on to heaven thou shalt go
in the *kitel* we shall sew.

"Come this way," said the rebbe. "We must watch the girls while you tell me about Sonia."

Lou followed the rebbe through an alcove into a small, dark room with a large window. The rebbe told Lou that they could watch the girls and hear them but that the girls did not know they were being observed.

"While you tell me Sonia's story, you must keep your eyes on the oldest girl. She is putting the finishing touches on Sonia's shroud and you must not take your eyes off her while you speak."

As she patiently stitched the flimsy white material, Lou began. "Her real name is Mogelonsky. She shortened it to Mogell when she came to Canada. She was born in Warsaw in 1932. During the war she lived inside the ghetto until it was no longer safe. Her parents took her and her sister, Rose, to Przewodowa. Of course, they knew they would never see their children again when they left them with the local priest, Father Joseph. After the war, Father Joseph arranged for the girls to live with a foster family in Black Heath, near London. Rose died soon after their arrival. Sonia was alone. In 1949, she obtained permission to immigrate to Canada as a war orphan sponsored by the Canadian Jewish Congress. She refused to be placed in another foster family. Our social worker at Congress tried to persuade her to change her mind but she assured them she could manage on her own.

"I feel responsible for her untimely death," Lou added. "The girl must have been desperate if she turned on the gas in her kitchen stove."

"Say the girl was desperate," instructed the rebbe. "It's important."

"She must have been desperate," Lou Greisman repeated.

"One never knows how our chosen suffer," the rebbe explained. "On the one hand, Sonia Mogelonsky satisfies all the martyr conditions; on the other hand, how can we be certain? Yet, my dear Mr. Greisman, with prayer and supplication we may actually open the gates of heaven. Let us bow our heads and pray."

The rebbe chanted in three languages, English, Yiddish, and

Aramaic. He closed his eyes and held his hands to his ears. His whole body rocked with such fervour that the room appeared to rock with him. "O Lilith," he cried, "you demoness, you witch, you temptress, why have you taken this young woman, our beloved Sonia Mogelonsky, from her earthly state?"

Lou felt a hot wind rise in the air about his neck. The eldest girl had thrown down Sonia's shroud. She danced wildly, picking up her long grey skirt, flaunting her grey bloomers and grey stockinged legs. The other girls joined her, while the rebbetzin, untouched by the spirit of the demoness, left the room.

The girls wailed. They begged: "Take us with you, Lilith. Don't let them cut our hair!" Suddenly they began tearing their grey cotton blouses, exposing their ripe, young breasts. By the end of their dance, they fell to the floor in a state of semi-consciousness.

The rebbe stood slowly, shaking his head in disbelief. "Poor Sonia Mogelonsky," he said to Lou. "The girl was under the spell of Lilith when she took her life. Lilith has told me everything. The demoness has confessed." Rebbe wiped the perspiration from his forehead. "Now," he announced, "the gates of heaven will open for our Sonia. Let us pray."

The girls next door slowly began to wake up. The rebbetzin returned carrying six fresh grey cotton blouses, one for each of them. She removed the torn ones while the girls dressed in silence as if they were drugged. Mendel Yehudah led Lou back to his study. The two men sat down exhausted.

"Sonia Mogelonsky is undoubtedly a martyr," said the rebbe. "But you can see, Mr. Greisman, how very difficult it is to wrest the spirit of a martyr from Lilith's spell." The rebbe rubbed his forehead. He ran his fingers through his unkempt beard.

Lou was sweating. "Where do we go from here, Rebbe?" he asked.

"We need more information," said Rebbe. "We need to know if Sonia had any close friends. A boyfriend?"

"No boyfriend," Lou deliberately lied.

"Then she was all alone in the world? You must tell the truth. It's very important for passage to *The World To Come.*"

Lou knew that Sonia had lived with Richard Vincennes for the last year. Nervous about his cover-up, he admitted, "There was a young man in her life, a fellow student at McGill. A French Canadian. But their relationship was platonic. After all, he was a Gentile," Lou emphasized. "The young man's name is Richard Vincennes. His parents, Claude and Isabelle, were very kind to Sonia. She used to visit them at their farm near Claremont-Ste Justine."

"But she did keep her distance from them?" Rebbe queried.

"Yes," Lou hesitated. "She was a wise girl. Always aware that the Vincennes were *Goyim.*"

Then, to Lou's great surprise, the rebbe announced, "She could have been closer to Richard Vincennes. Relationships with Gentiles do not count when the time comes for consideration of a Jewish soul to enter *The World To Come.*"

Lou was certainly relieved to hear the rebbe say this. Still, he was careful not to divulge details concerning Sonia and Richard's affair.

"The Vincennes are philanthropists, are they not?" asked the rebbe.

"Yes," said Lou Greisman. "The Vincennes can afford to be generous. They are ancestral owners of the old Barbienne seigneurie and run a profitable beef and slaughterhouse operation on the farm. Their son Richard was a childhood asthmatic. He spent months in the *Hotel Dieu.* The Vincennes have been most generous in their patronage of the hospital."

Rebbe nodded. "You think the Vincennes might consider contributing to the Datschlaver cause."

"I doubt it, rebbe. They have their own preferences when it comes to charities." But, he said, "I'll gladly make a personal donation to the Datschlavers."

"Then I assure you, Mr. Greisman, the girl will be taken care of."

Lou shook hands with the rebbe. "We'll all be taken care of, eh Rebbe?"

"Make sure Sonia's body gets here this afternoon, no later than five. No outsiders can come to the funeral. Only Datschlavers."

"Whatever you want, Rebbe," Lou said. "Shall I give a cheque to the beadle on my way out?"

"For the usual?" asked the rebbe.

"More," said Lou. "Ten thousand dollars."

"That's very generous, Mr. Greisman. The Datschlavers thank you."

3

The Vincennes waited for Lou Greisman in the Maritime Bar at the Ritz, Claude and Isabelle eating a lunch of grilled sole, Richard sipping chablis. What did Lou Greisman want at a time like this, Richard wondered?

Looking harassed, Greisman arrived at two-thirty, immediately ordering a double scotch. He didn't know how to begin, how to tell Richard about his decision to have the Datschlavers bury Sonia. He was afraid Richard would insist on attending the funeral. Because of the arrangements Lou had made with Mendel Yehudah, this was impossible. To further complicate matters, Richard was Sonia's next of kin on all her official forms, a fact which Lou had concealed from Mendel Yehudah.

Lou began the only way he knew how, abruptly, pointing out the distance that had always existed between Richard and Sonia because Richard wasn't Jewish. She was, after all, a Holocaust survivor. Richard was visibly shaken. Certainly

Lou was not the most tactful fellow. He spoke too directly. Now he crowned his pronouncements. "I'll give it to you straight, Richard. You can't attend Sonia's funeral."

"What the hell . . . ?"

"Cool it," Lou Greisman interrupted, "I'm not finished yet. I need you to sign this hospital release giving Congress the right to bury Sonia as we see fit."

Standing quickly, gritting his teeth, Richard was ready to strike Lou. Isabelle grabbed her son's sleeve, trying to restrain him. "Let go, Mother." Richard stared at Lou. "You manipulating sonofabitch. I'm tired of your interference. I'm tired of the literature your precious Jewish Congress keeps sending Sonia . . . kept sending." He broke off. "I am sick and tired of the words, *Holocaust survivor*. At least she is free from all that."

"Please calm down, son," said Claude. "Lou isn't the entire Canadian Jewish Congress. He's just the President."

"Which means nothing," said Lou, "because our people are all presidents." Lou cracked a smile.

"Is this a time for jokes?" asked Richard. "I've had it. I'm going to the hospital."

"I wouldn't do that if I were you," Lou said. "Sonia's suicide is more complicated than you think."

"Please son, listen to Lou," Richard's mother urged. He sat down slowly, his face pale with disappointment and sadness. He poured himself some more wine. He took a long sip. How cool the wine felt in his mouth, burning with anger. Sonia's body cold for less than twenty-four hours and here he was arguing with Lou Greisman about a funeral service.

"You have got to trust me," said Lou. "You know how long your father and I have been friends. I've arranged the best for Sonia. She's to be buried by the most pious Jews in the city. The Hasidim." He didn't say which sect. But he did add, "It is necessary. For her soul."

"What kind of crap . . . ?"

"Hang on," warned Greisman. "I know all about Sonia's

pregnancy. She came to see the Congress social worker."

"I should have known. Some silly bitch told her to have an abortion."

"Richard, please try to understand. The Hasidim don't know about you and Sonia. They think your relationship was platonic. If they knew about the abortion, I am certain they would refuse to bury her. And they must bury her, Richard." Lou hesitated, before he confided to Richard. "A week before her suicide, she wrote a letter which she gave to the Congress social worker, a letter she requested not be opened until yesterday. Her last request, Richard, was that the Hasidim bury her."

"But why?"

"You know she was a deeply religious person. Maybe she thought if the Hasidim buried her she would be ensured a life after death, especially since she decided to take her own life, which is against Jewish law."

Richard nodded uncomfortably. "Tell me what you want me to do."

"Come over to the hospital and sign the release papers. Promise not to show up at the funeral. Because of the suicide, the rebbe doesn't want any outsiders present."

"Should we go to the hospital with Richard?" Isabelle asked.

"It's better if Richard and I go alone," said Lou.

On the way to the hospital in Lou's limousine, Richard remembered walking along the same downtown streets with Sonia. He could feel her presence more powerfully now than when she was alive. For the first time since he had seen the ambulance outside their rooming house two nights ago, he felt strangely relieved. He could remember what he wanted about her and forget what he wanted too. At last he was in complete control.

After signing the papers at the hospital, Richard shook hands with Lou. "At least Sonia will have the funeral she wanted."

"Can I drive you home?" Lou asked.

"No thanks. I'd rather walk."

4

"This will be fine," said Richard, looking out the living room window, facing the courtyard and the Charles River. "Just fine," his voice taking on a singing leap. If only he could have followed it to the lower balcony on the right. Blonde, kinky curls, parted in the middle, two sets of waves dipping down to her shoulders, breasts the quality of the firmest white grapefruit, peeled, in contrast to her deep tan, her yellow-flowered bikini top swinging over the arm of the chaise lounge, pink nipples pointing to the August sun.

She was wearing the bikini bottom.

"Are there many students in this apartment, Mrs. Henderson?"

"Only students, Mister Vincennes," snapped the superintendent's wife. "This is Boston. You didn't expect to find an old lady on that balcony, did you?" Mrs. Henderson knew her female tenants had a habit of sunbathing topless. She guessed that Richard's glued position at the glass doors leading to his balcony was a sign he had caught a glimpse of some co-ed's bare skin. She thought quickly, for there were only two floors in the square building overlooking the Charles. Rona Bloom. She was probably out there sunning in her underpants. Mrs. Henderson scooted over to the window. "This is a respectable building, I'll have you know, Mr. Vincennes."

"I'm sure it is, Mrs. Henderson," Richard smiled.

Mrs. Henderson's two piece grey cotton suit puckered while she spoke. "What you need, Mrs. Henderson, if you don't mind my saying so, is a vest to go with that nice Sunday suit of yours."

"You young rascals are all the same," said Mrs. Henderson, showing all the superiority her sixty-two years could muster in the face of this summer silliness. "You'll be down to work, soon enough."

"Speaking of which, I'll need a better desk lamp. Can you get me another?"

"There's a variety of extra furniture in the basement. You'll find one there. Just get the key from Rona Bloom."

"Who's she?"

"Miss Pretty, who else?" Mrs. Henderson glanced towards the lower right balcony. "Now, you'll get the opportunity to see her with her top on."

"How lucky can a man get?"

"Here's your apartment key," Mrs. Henderson continued, "and here's another key for the front door. It's always locked after ten. I trust all is satisfactory, Mister Vincennes?"

"Just one more question. Can you introduce me to Miss Bloom? I'd like to get down to my studies this evening. Certainly could use that lamp," Richard squinted.

Mrs. Henderson marched down the hall in front of Richard, her matronly heels clicking. She knocked on Rona Bloom's door.

"What can I do for you, Mrs. Henderson?" Rona smiled cordially.

"I have a new tenant for number twelve, Mr. Vincennes." Mrs. Henderson nodded at Richard. "He needs a desk lamp. Can you take him down to the storage room in the basement?"

"I'm sorry, but I'm sunning now."

"Mrs. Henderson," Richard interrupted, "I certainly don't want to disturb Miss Bloom."

"Never mind," Mrs. Henderson said to Richard.

"Look, Miss Bloom it's four-thirty in the afternoon. How much sun can you get at this time of day? You get into something decent and help this studious young man get what he needs. I don't deduct five dollars a month off your rent for sunning," she declared.

Rona quickly slipped a pink terry shift over her golden shoulders.

"You have a smashing tan, Miss Bloom," said Richard, admiring her slender legs shown off to their best advantage by her backless high heeled pumps.

"Are you a student?" he asked.

"Art History, B.U. Third Year. And you?"

"I'm at Harvard Business School," Richard replied.

"My father would approve," she smiled widely.

"Would he? Why?" Richard asked.

"He's the senior partner at Harrison, Dunlop and Bloom, the largest manufacturer of farm equipment in the world," she blushed, embarrassed for having bragged. Quickly, she changed the subject. "My brother went to Harvard Business School but he dropped out after six months and moved to Israel. His one concession to my father. Daddy's an ardent Zionist, Mr. Vincennes."

"Miss Bloom, I don't wish to talk about your father or your brother. I would much rather talk about you." Richard paused, waiting for her to respond. When she didn't, he asked, "How does a beautiful young woman like you occupy herself when she's not sunning?"

"Let's get that lamp of yours," she smiled, not answering him.

In the storage room Richard put his hand gently on Rona's shoulder. "Will you have supper with me tonight? I was planning to work, but I couldn't concentrate, not after meeting you."

"I was going to have dinner alone. Maybe you would like to join me? I make the best omelette in Boston," she said impishly.

"What time?" Richard asked.

"Seven."

"I'll be there. On the button. I couldn't keep you waiting, Miss Bloom. You are so beautiful." He stared into her bright blue eyes where he saw only a slight amount of mischief and very little disappointment. She stared back, noticing the crow's feet at the corners of his. "I bet you read a lot," she said.

"Constantly. And you?"

"Not as much as I would like to." Her lips parted as he passed his fingertips across her smile.

"Seven," she reminded him, skipping ahead, her pink shift rising above the edge of her flowered bikini. What a lovely ass, Richard thought. And he quickly put his hands into his pants pockets to prevent his reaching out and pinching. He hardly knew Rona Bloom.

The smell of garlic butter greeted him when he arrived punctually at seven. Rona was still wearing her pink terry shift, and he guessed that only the flimsy bikini he had seen earlier was under it. He handed her a bouquet of fresh daisies.

"Classy," said Rona, picking up her shift near the top of her right thigh. "See, the flowers match."

Richard raised his eyebrows in approval. He wore a three piece off-white linen suit, a powder blue shirt with a stiff white collar and a Harvard tie. "I would like you to know I dressed especially for this occasion."

"Then, I better change too," Rona said.

"You don't have to."

"Of course, I do," she replied. Ten minutes later she returned wearing a white cotton skirt and scoop-necked blouse, her tan accentuated by the attire, her blonde hair tied back with a white, satin ribbon.

"You look angelic," Richard teased. "Quite virginal."

"I am a virgin," she answered flatly.

"A good looking woman, like you. You must wear a suit of armour beneath that skirt and blouse of yours."

"Just my bikini," she giggled, as she poured two glasses of *Pouilly Fuissé*, handing Richard a glass. "Father's favourite," she said, before mimicking his gruff voice. " '*Pouilly Fuissé* is the only wine served at Madame Romaine de Lyon's, the best omelette restaurant in New York.' " Then, she sweetly added, "Harrison, Dunlop and Bloom's main offices are in The Big

Apple. Ten floors in the Empire State Building."

"Congratulations," said Richard. "Now, how about forgetting your father and drinking to us." He took a long, slow sip. "I'm partial to *Pouilly Fuissé* myself. I have it often at home in Montreal."

"You're a Canadian?"

"I thought you would never get around to asking," Richard replied. "Our family farm is north of Montreal, close to the twin towns of Claremont-Ste Justine. Coincidentally, my father buys all our farm equipment from Harrison, Dunlop and Bloom."

"Small world," said Rona, adjusting her white hair ribbon.

"Our world, Miss Bloom. Shall we drink to our world?"

Rona's glass clinked with Richard's. Her nose curled as she sniffed the bouquet. Suddenly, she rushed away. "The garlic butter is burning." Moments later, long enough not to face Rona's burnt butter and an embarrassed woman, Richard glided into the kitchen, sitting on a stool at the counter where she was chopping mushrooms. She popped one into his mouth.

After their omelettes, they devoured strawberries served in thick glass brandy snifters. She poured spilts of champagne over the berries, then spooned in whipped cream. They drank the balance of the *Pol Roger Brut*. "Would you like to dance?" Richard asked.

He took her in his arms, leading her in small circles, before drawing his hands from her back to her breasts. Looking into her eyes, he gradually lifted her scoop-neck blouse over her shoulders. Beneath the bikini top, her nipples felt hard, about to burst beneath his fingers. They're daring me, he thought, as he pushed them inward, but they remained firm.

Rona reached for Richard's eyeglasses. She let her fingers caress his eyelids, kissing them open so that she looked directly into his cloudy blue eyes. She led him into her bedroom.

"I want you to leave on your white skirt," he said as he slowly undressed in front of her. A grimace came over his face, which drained to whiteness while a sickly perspiration formed on his forehead.

Rona was surprised. Although his sex was exceptionally large, he had no erection. "You must keep your skirt on," he repeated. "But reach under and pull off your bikini bottom. Do that now," he ordered.

She did not move. His harsh tone frightened her. She watched his hands. They seemed to grow, instead of his sex. "I'll take the bikini off," he said, as he reached under her skirt. "You've never wanted anything you couldn't have, have you?" he said sharply.

Trembling, she replied, "No, not until now. Now, I want you." But his sex still drooped. "I don't want to mark you," he said, lifting her across his knees. He raised her skirt back over her hips and slowly began spanking her. Gently at first, then harder. "Why are you doing this to me?" she cried out. He did not answer. After five minutes of hard slapping when her buttocks were hot and crimson, he made love to her.

5

The roses on Rona's bedroom walls were arranged in clumps of five, strategically shimmering from the silken, white wallpaper, a large ubiquitous rose dominating in the middle of each bouquet, the rest subservient.

But in the garden the roses were real, their pungent sweetness overwhelming on this unusually hot September day. The garden was long and narrow with each grassy blade severely manicured. A flagstone path with several archways adorned with roses climbing in and out of the white wood lattice led to a shady spot where Rona's parents sat comfortably, enjoying the outdoors.

Dressed in the same white blouse and skirt she had worn on her first date with Richard, Rona's hair hung loose, without a ribbon. Her straw hat with a red chiffon scarf tied around the rim flattened her blonde curls. Freckles proliferated on her face from her summer sunbathing. Mrs. Bloom wore a pale yellow, linen suit. A fresh yellow rose washed with orange was pinned to her jacket lapel. Her dark brown hair frosted with silver-beige strands appeared brittle in the sunlight.

Rona flopped down on the lawn near her parents. She nodded to Richard to join her.

"Now, Rona dear, bring this young man a chair or he'll ruin his suit."

"I'll get the chairs," said Richard. Instantly Rona leaped to her feet. "We won't have our guests do a thing," she said, imitating her mother's voice. Richard wished Rona's parents weren't about their beautiful garden. He wanted to make love to their daughter here among the roses.

Rona returned with two folding chairs. Richard opened both, dusting them carefully with his handkerchief that he removed from his inside jacket pocket. His outer jacket pocket, however, still sported a neatly folded hankie. Walter Bloom acknowledged Richard's fastidiousness. "Always carry two hankies myself," he said, handing Richard a wine glass filled with liquid and crushed strawberries. A slice of orange and a sprig of fresh mint floated on top. "Made it myself," he boasted. "Walter's punch. Would you like the recipe?"

"Don't go giving away any of your secrets, Mr. Bloom," Richard replied.

"For a fine chap like yourself . . . why not? Moselle," he continued, "that's the secret, and quality champagne. *Pol Roger*, 1954. Dubonnet, a splash, for that rich red colour. After all, the berries are red," he chuckled.

"*A votre santé*," said Richard, imbibing slowly. "This is delicious, Mr. Bloom. Any chance you could write out that secret for me?"

"Hey, Freda, did you hear that? When did David ever ask me to write out anything?"

"David?" Richard asked. He had forgotten Rona had a brother.

"Our son," said Freda. "He's not living with us any more."

"Oh, yes, Rona told me he lives in Israel."

"Yes," said Freda, dabbing her eyes with her yellow handkerchief.

"She misses him," said Walter. "But I don't. Used to drive me crazy. Always loafing. Never studying. I gave him the best. Understand? Sent him to Harvard Business School. And what does he do? Flunks out. You know what he's doing now? He grows avocados on a *moshav* near Tiberias. And he's twenty-nine. Not even married," Walter Bloom hastened to add.

"He may not like women, Daddy," Rona suggested, grinning at Richard.

Gradually, Richard drained his pink drink. "I'm sure everything will work out, Mr. Bloom. Your son is doing useful work."

"Somebody's got to do that sort of thing, I suppose. What can I do? I have a *farmer* for a son. Ironic, isn't it? My firm, Harrison, Dunlop and Bloom, the biggest manufacturer of farm equipment in the world, and my son drives a tractor on an avocado farm."

"Please Walter," Freda interjected, "Richard isn't interested in David."

"*Excusez Madame*," he deliberately used his French, wanting to sound more genuine, "I don't mind."

"Thank you," Mr. Bloom said. "I only wanted the best for David," he continued, putting down his drink on the top tier of the wrought iron and glass garden table. On the bottom tier rested assorted bottles of gin, vodka, scotch, and bourbon. "How about something a little stronger than Walter's punch?

You like bourbon?'' he asked, addressing only Richard, who nodded.

"Well sir, what are we waiting for?" asked Walter Bloom. He poured two bourbon, handing one to Richard, and directing him to the path, leading to the back garden. "We'll be back in half an hour," he announced to Freda and his daughter. "In time for lunch. I'm hungry as a bear."

"Lunch in half an hour," Freda obediently repeated. Rona burned every time her mother yielded to her father's whims, yet she marched as quickly as Freda back to the house.

"I ordered sole for lunch," Mrs. Bloom said to Rona. "And fiddleheads from New Brunswick."

"I adore fiddleheads," said Rona, suffering from a perpetually ravenous appetite. Freda was always warning her daughter about gaining weight while Walter Bloom would interrupt, saying, "Really, Freda, Rona is a healthy, young woman."

"I'm starved," Rona announced to her mother. "What else are we having?"

"Cold cream of watercress to start ..."

"M-m-m."

"Some of cook's cheddar cheese dreams; sliced tomato and Belgian endive salad with lemon parsley dressing ... "

"And dessert?" asked Rona.

"You're actually considering dessert, young woman, after a meal like that ... your figure ... "

Rona smiled. "You like Richard, don't you?"

"Yes, and so does your father. You can tell," she paused, puttering with the roses she had brought in from the garden, arranging them carefully for the dining room table centre piece. "And why shouldn't he like him? You can see the young man is well brought up. He knows how to behave, what to say. He is impressive, Rona."

"Daddy's betting on him already, that's obvious," said Rona.

"Just remember," warned Mrs. Bloom, "he's not Jewish."

"That's not what I'm referring to. Daddy's interested in Richard for business purposes, isn't he?"

"You mustn't talk that way about your father, as if he treats people like property. Naturally, he likes to meet ambitious, young men, especially if they're intelligent. Maybe Father will give Mr. Vincennes a break. He ought to be appreciative, my dear girl."

"Yes, Mother, I guess you're right. Will you excuse me while I run up and change?"

Rona went to her room feeling totally aroused. She slipped out of her white skirt and blouse into a pink, sleeveless sundress. While she adjusted the off-the-shoulder top, she squeezed her legs together in anticipation of Richard who after the fish lunch would be hers alone. Rona had slept with him several times. With a particular sense of female pride she recalled the intensity of his love-making. She thought about the spanking on the first night they made love. She could feel Richard's strong hands stinging her bottom as she changed into a pair of pink silk stockings, pulling them slowly up her slender legs, looking over her shoulder into the closet mirror in order to fasten her back garters. She still had a bruise at the base of her right buttock. She passed her fingers gently over the blue-grey mark.

"So, Mr. Vincennes, it's very simple," said Walter Bloom, as he accidentally flicked cigar ash into his private pond filled with speckled trout. He grinned with embarrassment as the trout leaped at the residue. "These trout of mine will bite anything, even a ripple. Like the young brides back 'ome, they are. Nervous. Jumpy." For a second, in his enthusiasm at seeing the trout jump, he dropped the 'h' in home. "In Hendon, the London suburb where I was born and raised, the poor man's Golder's Green, people often drop their 'h's."

"My father was the *shul shammos*. Nothing more than a glorified janitor. He was a *shabbos Goy*, too. That's right, he worked on Saturdays, on the Jewish Sabbath! *Goy* is not slang," he hastened to clarify. "It means *nation*, the other nations, them as opposed to us: *The Chosen*. You know how the story goes. I'm just giving you a bit of background, so you'll understand this Rona of ours."

He sat down on one of the benches at the end of the pond. Richard joined him.

"I think you ought to know, I'm not a religious man," Bloom confessed. "My parents were hardworking people. I helped both of them. My mother was the synagogue caterer, a *berye*, and my father, he cleaned while she cooked and I ran between them collecting plates and prayerbooks," Bloom chortled. He considered himself a man who could amuse especially with a turn of phrase.

Richard listened carefully, smiling now and then.

"The other kids at the synagogue looked down on me," said Walter bitterly. "But, to my parents, I was a jewel. Their only son, like our David." He paused to ponder.

"They scrimped for me. Sent me to study Economics at LondonUniversity. Nothing but the best for their Walter. Naturally, I was grateful. Every summer I worked to help pay my tuition.

"Harrison and Dunlop. From the beginning I worked for them. At the main plant in Surrey where they manufactured and tested their farm equipment. Near Wimbledon. A small town called Sutton. They had a huge model farm for testing their tractors. Those red ones they used to be famous for.

"I was spending my first summer with them when they made their big discovery. A self propelled tractor that could reap as well as thresh. Instead of being drawn by horses, it was mounted on a chassis. Immediately I suggested to the foreman that Harrison and Dunlop change the colour of its tractors from red to green, our competitor's colour, whose tractors by the way could accomplish only half of what ours could. Soon we were outselling him four to one."

Impressed, Richard raised his eyebrows. Walter Bloom offered him a cigar, but Richard, a non-smoker, declined.

"Don't mind if I have another, do you?" he asked Richard.

"No, not at all. I enjoy the smell of a superior cigar."

Walter Bloom grinned proudly. "The summer had just begun

and my ideas were flowing like a gushing reservoir. I organized demonstrations of our new tractor all over England. In the past, the firm had brought blokes from as far away as Manchester and Liverpool without their families. But I knew better. Let them bring the wife and kiddies, make a memorable occasion of their visit to Harrison and Dunlop's model farm."

"Sound's like a good idea," said Richard.

"Good? It was great!" declared Walter Bloom. "We gave them dinners, dancing, live entertainment from London. Once we brought in Maurice Chevalier. He told those farmers that if he could live his life over again, he wouldn't go into the entertainment business; he'd rather homestead with a fleet of Harrison and Dunlop tractors.

"It worked," Walter said excitedly. "The hoop-la. The hard-sell. They went crazy for those tractors. The salesmen couldn't keep up with the orders. Of course, back then, Harrison and Dunlop was only English and American. But one success led to another. By the time I left London University, we had our first big European plant. At Le Havre." Walter's mouth watered. "I was an ambitious young man," he said, "full of ideas. I saw my golden opportunity when I first met Frederick Harrison."

"Where did you meet him? I thought these corporate fellows rarely left their boardrooms," Richard said.

"You can be certain I didn't meet Frederick Harrison in my father's synagogue. We met at St. Martin's-in-the-Fields Church at one of the noon hour concerts. An unknown male pianist was playing Grieg concertos. A superb performance. By sheer coincidence, Frederick Harrison was sitting next to me. We began to chat in the interval, commenting on the young man's virtuosity. 'Talent among the young is both rare and beautiful. Exciting too,' Harrison said to me."

Richard nodded, "Obviously a very forthcoming gentleman."

"Forthcoming is exactly what Frederick Harrison was. Wait

until you hear the rest. We walked out of the church together and Harrison is still talking. 'I like encouraging new, young talent,' he tells me. 'Why?' I ask him. 'Discovery,' he says candidly. 'In my business, discovery is the name of the game.' Soon, we're eating lunch at The Dorchester, paper thin slices of grilled liver with crisp bacon. Naturally I pushed the bacon aside. We Jews don't eat bacon. You know that.''

''Yes, I know. I dated a Jewish girl when I was a student at McGill.''

''And our Rona,'' Bloom nodded, ''well, why not. Just because you date them, doesn't mean you're going to marry them.''

Richard shrugged, giving Walter Bloom a sly smile. He eagerly continued where he had left off. ''We had coffee and cigars in Harrison's Dorchester suite. He always stayed at The Dorchester when he was in London. After two Remy Martins, I learned I had landed myself a summer job for the rest of my years at the University of London. I was still in my first year. 'Bloom,' Harrison said to me, 'we'll keep a job open for you every summer as long as you promise to work for us when you graduate.'

''I told him my plans for a Master's degree at Harvard Business School. 'After your Master's, sir,' he corrected himself. He shook my hand so hard I thought it would fall off. 'You damn well better not disappoint me,' he said.

''It was as easy as that. The beginning of my corporate climb to the Vice Presidency of one of the world's largest multinational companies. Hard to believe, isn't it?''

''Yes, sir, it is.''

''Richard, what would you say if I were to offer you the same kind of opportunity. We could start with you working in our Waltham plant next summer. You could see how you like the business and we would have the opportunity to get better acquainted.''

''I'd be delighted to work for Harrison, Dunlop and Bloom, sir. My academic adviser suggested I seek summer employment. You have saved me the trouble of looking. I'm grateful. But, excuse me, Mr. Bloom, didn't you want to tell me about your daughter? You said earlier on in our conversation that you wanted me to understand her better."

"A bit of background, Richard, that's all," said Walter Bloom, as he led Richard back up the garden path towards the house.

In the Florida room overlooking the garden they were all seated around a kidney-shaped mahogany dining table, Walter and Freda Bloom at the centre, Richard and Rona opposite each other.

"Please pass the fish, Rona, and some of that dill sauce of your mother's. My wife is a fabulous cook," Walter Bloom boasted. "I'd like you to know, Richard, she never follows a recipe. Right, dear?" He turned to his wife who was sitting on his right.

"Walter, I didn't make the sauce. Sara did."

"Sara?"

"Yes, Walter, Sara! Don't act so surprised."

"But, Darling, I'd know your dill sauce anywhere."

Richard watched Mrs. Bloom shrug, push the last of her sole closer to the sauce. "Sara learned by watching me." Mrs. Bloom leered unhappily in Rona's direction.

"My mother is devoted to her family. To father and me. David, as you have already learned, is no longer with us." Richard detected a tone of rebellion in Rona's voice. "Soon, I, too, will be on my own," she hastened to add.

"I've had quite enough from you, young lady," said Mrs.

Bloom. "It's my absolute pleasure to please my family. Maybe I do go out of my way to see this is accomplished, but nothing in this house happens in a minute, my dear girl, as you seem to think." Freda Bloom pulled out her yellow hankie, folded in a neat cone, from the breast pocket of her linen jacket. She dabbed the tears trickling down her face. "At least in our home, routine is handled as if it were art."

A broad grin appeared on Walter Bloom's face.

"Now, Mother, that's the crowning insult," said Rona. "You really know how to dish it out. In a minute you'll be asking Richard if he doesn't agree with you? You'll inquire about his mother. 'Is your mother traditional, Mr. Vincennes, or is she one of the liberated types?' "

"I don't have a word to add," interjected Mrs. Bloom, picking up her cue. "Frankly, dear, you've covered everything."

"There, didn't I tell you?" Rona asked, looking across to Richard for support. At first he didn't speak, took his time finishing his fiddleheads and perked up his eyebrows when Manny arrived with the endive salad.

"Rona, I think your parents have a point. It's wonderful for a modern woman like yourself to have a career, but you should also give yourself the opportunity to be somewhat domestic-minded." Immediately, he could feel the tension seed itself in the room.

"I'll have you know, Mr. Vincennes," Rona retaliated, her dark brown eyes wildly reproachful, "I am bloody domestic-minded. But I'm also bloody business-minded. Why do you think I'm taking a degree in Fine Art? Because college will do more for Rona Bloom than teach her how to pick paintings for her Brookline living room. Boston University is offering extensions courses in business to its art students. I plan to enroll in all of them."

Walter Bloom beamed. Here was a practical woman. Alas, she was truly his daughter. Certainly more sensible than her idealistic brother.

Rona continued, obviously gaining confidence from the lack

of interruption. "I'm going to open my own gallery on New-bury Street. I plan to carry old masters and contemporary art-ists from all over the world." Rona stared purposefully at her father. "With my dear Father's generous and able assistance . . ."

"You're talking about the capital to get started I assume?" Walter Bloom asked.

"Naturally," she replied, but Richard could see this lively girlfriend of his had even more on her entrepreneurial mind. "I'll need your connections, Father. To be specific, I'm deter-mined to be an international success, even if success means sacrificing family life." Nobody commented.

A dark thought tucked its way into Richard's mind as he remembered Walter Bloom's treatment of his wife and daugh-ter earlier in the garden. Reluctant to discuss business in their presence, he had dismissed them, hurrying Richard to the fish pond. Richard thought of his own mother, an antithesis to the Bloom women. Reticent by nature, her conversation usually centered around activities sponsored by the Claremont-Ste Justine church, suppers for the poor and her ladies sewing circle, famous for their quilts and tapestries.

Richard decided it was his mother's deeply rooted humility which contrasted so markedly with the strong egocentricity of Rona and her mother. Mrs. Bloom disagreed with her daughter's choice of vocation, emphasizing her own entre-preneurial bent for the running of the Bloom household. Except for the pond filled with trout and the bottom tier of the wrought iron tea cart stacked with liquor bottles sitting in the rose garden, Richard had seen little evidence of Walter Bloom's presence on the premises. Still, Richard concluded that his host wasn't suffering from authority deprivation.

It was almost two in the afternoon and Richard and Rona had to leave if they were to get to the Gardner Museum for the mid-afternoon concert they had planned to attend. Walter invited Richard to lunch the following Sunday. Freda instant-ly informed him that the Blooms always had special Sunday lunches. "Do you have any favourite foods, Mr. Vincennes?" she coyly asked. "Perhaps Rona will make something you're particularly fond of."

"Mother," Rona said heatedly, "I cook for Richard in my own apartment. Remember, he lives just one floor down from me.

"I thought you two just met a few weeks ago," said Mrs. Bloom.

"That's right, Mother, but we enjoy each other's company, so we've often been having our meals together," Rona smiled, pecking her mother on the forehead. "Times are changing, Mother," she grinned, before giving her father the manliest handshake she could muster. "Dad," she said boldly, "we'll discuss this gallery of mine soon, I hope."

"Whenever you like Rona, dear."

"We better get going," Richard said, taking her firmly by the arm. "Thank you for lunch, Mrs. Bloom, and for the invitation for next week," he said to his host. Walter Bloom motioned for Richard to step aside. He whispered softly, "Remember, Harrison, Dunlop and Bloom's offer for next summer is strictly confidential."

"Yes," Richard answered, before he said goodby.

Eighteen months later Richard was packing his bags for Paris. The summer of his college interim year at Harrison, Dunlop and Bloom's Waltham plant had been extraordinarily successful. Having observed Richard on the job, Walter Bloom was convinced that the young French Canadian was exactly the man needed for head office in Paris. Then Richard stood first in his class. Walter was proud of his intuition.

Rona came to see Richard in his apartment before his departure for France. It was a hot June day and she wore the same yellow-flowered bikini and pink terry shift she had worn during their first meeting. "Want to come up to my place. There are a few important matters I think we ought to discuss and I'll feel more comfortable on my own turf." Her lips moved from a coy smile to a dissatisfied pout, an increasingly familiar look to Richard. He refused to take on her morose mood. "I've been seriously contemplating whether I shall ever lay eyes on such a lovely ass again," he said as he gave her a friendly pat on the buttocks. Then he drew her close and kissed her firmly on the mouth.

"This isn't goodbye," said Rona. "I'm coming to Paris in August. Looking for the perfect bottom in the Louvre," she tried to lighten the scene.

"I thought you had your work cut out for you here in Boston, setting up your own art gallery. What the hell are you coming to Paris for?" he said, showing his displeasure. He had hoped to put a freeze on their affair, thinking the new job provided the perfect opportunity.

"I need to immerse myself in the works of the great masters. I'm also going to London and Rome. I thought, Richard Vincennes, you'd be pleased about my trip. If you'd rather I didn't call you when I get to Paris, okay by me. I'll just gallery hop by myself." End of coyness, on to her business voice. She could switch back and forth as quickly as his first great love, Sonia Magell. What is it about these Jewish women? Richard thought to himself.

"At least two weeks in the *Louvre*," Rona continued, "three days devoted to the *Jeu de Paumes*, a day for the *Musée Rodin*, a side trip to Versailles and Fountainbleu, not to mention a week set aside for buying at the small private galleries. Daddy has arranged for Harrison, Dunlop and Blooms' Paris company's president, your new boss, to make all the necessary introductions."

"You better watch out," said Richard, "I hear M. Perrain is a womanizer, particularly fond of women in their twenties with blonde, kinky curls."

On the balcony in Rona's apartment they sipped vodka martinis. Rona babbled incessantly about business while Richard became more and more aroused, especially when she imitated her father: " 'Since I can't help finance the avocado industry in Israel, I may as well help you get a line of credit

to bring art of international significance to Boston.' '' Rona
stuck out her chest while she spoke. As if the sun could tan
those dark nipples of hers, Richard thought, for she had taken
off her bikini top. He put down his martini glass on the
windowledge and walked over behind her chair. He reached
down with one hand, taking each of her nipples in turn
between his fingers, manipulating them as if he were a pencil
sharpener. With his other hand he began spanking her, lightly
at first, then harder. She begged him to stop. He did, turning
away momentarily to undo his belt. ''Bend over the railing of
the balcony,'' he said, ''I want to pay hommage to your ass one
last time.''

7

It was in 1961 that the Datschlaver rebbe of Montreal first
contacted Claude Vincennes to ask him if he would consider
selling his farm near Claremont-Ste Justine to the Datschlaver
Hasidim.

''Hey-lo, Mister Vin-seen, you don't know me. Mine name
is Kasarkofski, Mendel Yehudah Kasarkofski, the Datschlaver
rebbe.'' His accent was a deliberate disguise. Born and raised
in Montreal he spoke impeccable English. But he usually
didn't make phone calls to Gentiles and therefore wished to
maintain an aura of secrecy about his person.

''What did you say your name was?'' Claude Vincennes
asked politely.

''The rebbeh! I am callink because I vish to meet mit you to
half some talkink about serious things.''

''I beg your pardon, Monsieur Kasark ... ''

''Kasarkofski,'' the rebbe helped him out.

"Monsieur Kasarkofski, if you can't tell me what you wish to discuss, I won't be able to meet with you." Trying to be patient, Vincennes added, "I don't even know you, sir."

"I tink you talkink vise, Mister Vin-seen. I send my helpeh to half talking mit you. Vy should two busy people like us be boddered mit talking? You get helpeh to speak mit mine helpeh. Tomorrow morning at eleven-thirty. Okay, Misteh?"

Claude was too intrigued to say no. "Where will they meet, Rabbi Kasarkofski?"

"In mine study in the Datschlaver *shtiebel*. 4067 Jeanne Mance."

"The *shtiebel*?" Vincennes repeated vaguely. He hadn't the slightest idea what a *shtiebel* was but he knew the street. It was in a Jewish section of town that he occasionally visited with his friend and business partner, Lou Greisman. Immediately, *shtiebel* rang familiar. Greisman had called the small synagogues in the neighbourhood *shtiebels*.

"My son will represent me," he told the rebbe. "Whom shall he ask for?"

"Who? Vy, Judah Leib, who else? Judah Leib, who is doing beeg beezniz for the Datschlavers. He will be waiting for your helpeh, Mister Vin-seen."

"Thank you for calling, Rabbi Kasarkofski."

"And vy are you tankink me now; vait until your helpeh hears, den you'll be tankink."

Claude couldn't help laughing. He held his hand over the mouth of the receiver before completing the call. "It's all arranged then. Goodbye, Rabbi."

The timing could not have been better. Richard was back in Montreal for the summer teaching an evening seminar at McGill for businessmen on investment in France. He had been thinking seriously about not returning to Paris where he had been working for the Boston-based multinational company Harrison, Dunlop and Bloom since his graduation from Harvard Business School.

On the same day that Claude Vincennes spoke with the

Datschlaver rebbe, Richard and his father joined Lou Greisman for dinner at the Café de Paris in the Ritz Carleton. After considerable persuasion from his father and Lou, Richard agreed to meet the Datschlavers' representative. The Hasidim in Montreal had always fascinated him. Concentrated in the enclaves of St. Urbain and St. Viatur, they rarely left those streets, appeared, in fact, to have a separate world in the middle of downtown Montreal. Lou explained that the Datschlavers were certainly the most zealous and eccentric Hasidic sect in the city. Unlike the Lubavitchers who welcomed Jewish converts to their sect, the Datschlavers shunned their fellow Jews as well as their fellow Hasidim. Only their rebbe had status and they worshipped him with a totally encompassing faith.

"Maybe these Datschlavers will present the challenge I have been looking for," Richard said, facetiously.

"You never know," said Lou. "They're a charismatic bunch!"

"You know them?" Richard asked.

"Lou knows everyone in the Jewish community," said Claude, convinced that his good friend, Lou Greisman, was responsible for the Datschlavers contacting him. He knew that Lou generously supported some of the Montreal Hasidim. There were at least five sects in the city.

At eleven-thirty the next morning when Richard rang the doorbell of the Datschlaver synagogue, no one answered. He sat down on the front porch to wait. Not until close to twelve did someone appear. Richard blinked to make sure he was seeing properly. A white lorrie with crimson curtains in the windows had pulled up to the curb and a short man in a dark blue business suit emerged.

"You must be Richard Vincennes," the man said, speaking impeccable English, without a trace of a Yiddish accent. He had unusual posture, his body tilting sideways while he held his head stiffly in the opposite direction so that he looked like a human seesaw. He turned to salute his chauffeur. Then he did an about face, saluting Richard. "Allow me to introduce myself," he said, "I'm Judah Leib, the slaughterer."

"Pleased to meet you," Richard paused, pondering the man's title. "Your rabbi told my father that the Datschlavers have some business to discuss with us."

"Yes, important business," he said, shaking Richard's hand. "Come," he motioned. "this way. I want you to meet my daughter, Faigele. Faigele means little bird," he explained.

"Really?" said Richard, raising his eyebrows, conjuring up a vision worthy of the name, while Judah Leib reached into his suit pocket for his key ring. "So many keys I have, Mister. This one here is for the St. Laurent abbatoir and this one here is for Epstein's *kosher* butcher shop on Victoria. Here is the key for the rebbe's study . . . it's upstairs." He pointed. "And here is the key I want!"

Judah Leib and Richard poked their way along a dim, musty corridor to a bright florescent-lit office. Three desks sat in the middle of the room and in front of them two rather worn red leather sofas. Judah Leib stationed himself at the centre desk. A woman was already seated on the sofa facing Judah Leib.

"Please, sit down, Mister Vincennes," he pointed to the empty sofa. "There, if you don't mind. Datschlaver women don't sit next to men," he announced, "except members of their immediate family. And then, only at certain times; in accordance with our laws, you understand?"

No, I don't, Richard thought to himself, yet he nodded.

"Faigele," said Judah Leib, "I would like you to meet Mister Vincennes. Mister Vincennes, this is my daughter, Faigele."

Judah Leib's little bird was incredibly beautiful. Judging from the length of her grey skirt descending from her slender waist to her ankles, he guessed her height to be about five feet, nine inches. She wore a grey cotton blouse covered by a matching crocheted sweater with cape sleeves. Her black hair, parted in the middle, pulled back simply by a satin ribbon, fell softly down her back. It seemed to him that she was waiting to have that ribbon untied.

Yes, he was definitely attracted to her. Without a drop of make-up and even in her drab attire, there was something unspoiled and fresh about her. Pink cheeks — he was certain she had pinched plenty to achieve their high colour before he and her father walked into the room. Not supposed to sit next to men, he smiled to himself. With all that glow on her face she may as well be sitting on his lap.

"Mister Vincennes, I'll get to the heart of the matter, if you don't mind."

"Please," urged Richard, as he kept his eyes fixed on Faigele.

Judah Leib began, "Perhaps you have read recently in the newspapers about our people?"

"Yes, in *The Gazette*. The Datschlavers want to leave Montreal because they are having difficulty maintaining their pious lifestyle. Is that right?"

"Listen, Mister Vincennes, I hope you don't mind me calling you, Mister, instead of *Monsieur*."

"If you prefer Mister, I don't mind."

"You're a kind man, Mister, I can see that. I'm very pleased to discuss the future of the Datschlaver Hasidim with a man such as yourself."

Richard nodded.

Judah Leib continued, "Let me tell you frankly, right here, in this room, with Faigele as my witness, the situation for our people is desperate. In one word I can tell you the problem: *Assimilation*. And it's not that our children are marrying Gentiles. If, you'll excuse me for being so blunt, they were to go off with Gentiles, we would know where we stand. But no, instead those Datschlavers who stray, waver continually between some other stream of Judaism and our own.

"Let me get to the point," Judah Leib said, while Richard began to wonder if this were possible. "Just last month the Datschlaver directorate met in Jerusalem at the Sheba Hotel. Do you know the Sheba?" he paused to ask Richard.

"Can't say that I do," Richard shrugged.

"Fancy, like you wouldn't believe. The chief Datschlaver

rebbe from the Mea Shearim arranged everything. All food was prepared with strict observance to Datschlaver dietary law, which is similar to the Orthodox but stricter. There are twenty-three foods eaten by Orthodox Jews that we don't touch and six foods that our sect alone eats. One recipe, stuffed dinney, the most popular of the six, was served every night."

Judah Leib smiled eagerly. "Let me tell you more about the conference. Altogether there were forty-eight delegates, twelve from each of the four Datschlaver communities in Jerusalem, London, New York, and Montreal. The Mea Shearim rebbe, Eliahu Kasarkofski, presided.

"Would you believe that he is having troubles in the Mea Shearim? Ultra Orthodox Jews won't leave each other alone. A group of Satmarers attacked a Datschlaver teenager, ripped off his beard and sidelocks with a butcher knife."

"But why?" Richard asked.

"Because the Datschlaver would not join their sect. Because he was unwilling to compromise a single aspect of Datschlaver Law. It's very simple," Judah Leib continued. "They will not leave us alone. After Reb Eliahu told his troubles, Reb Benjamin from London related his.

"Mister Vincennes, it's the same for *all* Datschlavers." He said this as if there were so many, yet their total numbers were less than one thousand world-wide. "We cannot live the way we want to. With the exception of our New York brethren." He paused. "And this is what I'm getting at."

At last, Richard thought, though he was fascinated by the slaughterer's story.

"In 1955 Williamsburg's Reb Moses moved his people out of the city to a location eight miles off an exit on the New York turnpike, an hour's drive from Williamsburg. For six years Reb Moses' Datschlavers have had peace. He has advised us to follow his example."

"The Datschlaver rabbis are very devoted to one another. Are they related?" asked Richard.

"Reb Moses, Reb Benjamin, and our Rebbe Mendel Yehudah

are brothers. Their father Shmuel was a brother to the Jerusalem Reb Eliahu's father, Ya'akov. Ya'akov and Shmuel were born to the good Rifkeh and Reb Reuben Kasarkofski in Datschlav, Poland in the 1880s."

Richard knew very little about the Datschlavers but the more he learned the more they intrigued him. "Would the Mea Shearim rebbe consider moving?" asked Richard.

"It won't be the first time we Jews have had to leave Jerusalem," answered Judah Leib.

"Where would he go?" Richard asked.

Until now, Faigele had contributed little to the meeting, but when Richard began asking questions, she began writing in her notebook. Richard wondered whether she was her father's secretary but he decided not to ask. She was there, but not there, as far as Judah Leib was concerned. While she wrote, her long, black hair swung round over her right shoulder. Richard was certain she was peeking at him out of the corner of her eye. She even seemed to have a half smile on her lips, as if she were thinking, "I'm not supposed to look at you but I want too."

Flirting? Not exactly. Rather, taking a risk. Yes, that was it. She was having a wonderful time doing what was forbidden. Her rebellion charmed him. He found himself more and more drawn to her.

Judah Leib continued. "Just the other day, the Jerusalem rebbe wrote to our Mendel Yehudah to say that he had purchased land ten miles south of the University of Beersheva. Fit for Bedouins and Datschlavers, free from corrupting influences. He pleaded with Mendel Yehudah to move his Montreal Datschlavers out of the city, too."

Richard now realized why he had been summoned. "You wish to buy land from my father? Am I right, Judah Leib?"

"Exactly what is on our minds," replied the slaughterer. "But first we wanted you to know some of our history."

"Very wise," acknowledged Richard, smiling at Faigele, who was still busy recording. "It's a coincidence, I'm sure, but my father has been thinking of selling our farm. He wants to move to Montreal. I, on the other hand, have had enough of big city life. I was hoping to move back permanently from Paris, to return to my father's land."

Judah Leib didn't seem to hear him. "Just to show you how serious we Datschlavers are, I have a cheque here for two hundred and fifty thousand dollars for ten hectares of your ancestor's Barbienne seigneurie. We will pay your father for everything, the land, the manor house, the servants' cottage, the barns, and even the slaughterhouse." Judah Leib's eyes gleamed as he mentioned the abbatoir. "Here, Mister Vincennes, have a look, the cheque is good, I assure you."

Richard examined it. Just a few weeks ago his father had mentioned two hundred and fifty thousand as a fair asking price for the property belonging to Richard's mother's family, the Barbeaus, since the 1700s. The Datschlaver offer appeared most enticing. Richard glanced at the other enticement, the beautiful Faigele. "We shall certainly consider your offer, Judah Leib," said Richard, "but I must tell you again, sir, I am not prepared to leave my family's land."

"Maybe we can make a deal, Mister Vincennes," said Judah Leib.

Richard thought that Faigele's face brightened considerably as she continued to record in her notebook.

"I'll tell you what I would like, Judah Leib. Some land for myself at the edge of your community. Close to the Laurentians would be my choice. I can show you if you have some paper."

Richard reached into his inside jacket pocket for his fountain pen. "I can draw the farm with my eyes closed," he told Judah Leib. While he drew, he explained, "In exchange for some land and the guarantee of a certain lifestyle, I shall agree to look out for the interests of your people." He paused, lifting his pen from the page, "You agree you will need some protection, living in the middle of the French-Canadian countryside?"

Judah Leib shrugged, looking over at Faigele to see if she was writing down everything Richard said. Later that evening Mendel Yehudah would want to read the exchange between Judah Leib and Richard Vincennes. "Protection, we have, Mister Vincennes, from *The Holy One Blessed Be He*."

"I realize you are deeply religious," Richard replied. "Still, you will be living among Gentiles. Only five miles away are the twin towns of Claremont-Ste Justine. How do you think the town's inhabitants will react when they learn that the new owners of the Vincennes farm are a community of Hasidim?"

"We won't bother them," Judah Leib said emphatically. "Everything we need, we'll be getting from Montreal."

"All the more reason for them to be suspicious."

"Maybe you have a point, Mister Vincennes. A little protection from a *Goy*, you should excuse the Yiddish expression, we could use. Now please, tell me more about this lifestyle of yours."

"Unlike the Datschlavers I must live in comfort."

"So, what is wrong with your father's house?"

"The manor is a beautiful residence but it is situated in the middle of the estate and I cherish my privacy."

"Ah, you wish to keep to yourself. That is good. The rebbe will like that."

"Why not please the rebbe?" Richard smiled at Faigele. She looked up from her notebook and smiled back. Her father did not see.

"However, I think you should know that it's not solely my desire for privacy that prevents me from moving into the manor," Richard continued. "You see, it's very old, as elegant an example of late 1800s architecture as you can find in Quebec farmhouses, but the rooms are small. There are alcoves everywhere and very little decent wall space. Hardly adequate for my needs. I have a large collection of paintings by contemporary artists and old masters. I need wall space in order to hang them."

"Excuse me, Mister Vincennes, you say you have paintings

by *old masters*?" Judah Leib's voice expressed surprise and wonder. He had no idea that some of the great Hasidic rebbes often referred to as *old masters* were artists. "I have never seen a painting by a rebbe," he mistakenly told Richard.

"Not by rebbes, Judah Leib," Richard tried to set the slaughterer straight. "The masters I am referring to are not necessarily Jewish, although two of my favourite paintings in my personal possession are by artists who happen to be Jewish, Amedeo Modigliani and Marc Chagall."

Judah Leib nodded hesitantly. With a sigh of relief, he said, "My son, Baruch, wants to be an artist. He draws beautifully and his handwriting is perfection. Rebbe Mendel Yehudah would have liked him to be a scribe but he has never applied himself properly to his *yeshiva* studies. Instead he doodles and daydreams."

"Artists are creators," Richard tried to explain to Judah Leib. "They need to dream. You and your people should be grateful for your son's talent. You should encourage him."

Judah Leib shook his head. "You don't understand. The rebbe cannot approve of Baruch's talent. But I don't want to talk about Datschlaver Law. Tell me more about art," Judah Leib asked anxiously.

"When I lived in Paris, I travelled all over Europe. I visited many many famous art galleries and museums. I made many purchases."

"My son, Baruch, would like to see your paintings," said Judah Leib. "As for myself, I'm not interested. Do you know Mister Vincennes, I have never been inside an art gallery?"

"Surely you have visited the Montreal Museum of Fine Arts on Sherbrooke?" Richard said. "It's almost around the corner."

"Never! We are not allowed to set foot in the place."

Richard couldn't believe what he was hearing. How could these Datschlavers, residing in the heart of Montreal, live such isolated lives? "I do not understand your people, Judah Leib."

"It's very simple. You have your ways. We have ours," he said. "If you wish to remain on your father's farm, it is not only better but absolutely necessary that you should live a respectable distance from our people."

Richard nodded before continuing, "In my home, I will also need space for my library."

"How many books do you have?" asked Judah Leib.

"Probably a few thousand. Only a very large home with three or four sitting rooms would be adequate to house both my books and paintings. Besides, the Datschlavers will likely want the manor for one of their main buildings because of its location."

Judah Leib tried to absorb everything Richard had told him. The Datschlavers too had lots of books, yet they found room for them in their crowded dwellings. But then, he thought to himself, we have only religious books. Judah Leib knew there were other books in the world, books prohibited by the chief Datschlaver rebbe in Jerusalem. Although he didn't understand why, he felt drawn to the Gentile, Richard Vincennes.

"How does my proposition sound, Judah Leib?" Richard inquired.

Judah Leib tried to convince Rebbe Mendel Yehudah that a successful slaughterhouse was as crucial to the Canadian Datschlavers' survival as their *yeshiva*.

In Montreal, Datschlavers earned their livings as teachers in small synagogues. Others were beadles, scribes, and ritual slaughterers. A few owned small shops. Still, day and night, these pious men found time to study and pray. If not for the donations of wealthy philanthropists like Lou Greisman, many a Datschlaver family would have gone hungry.

That's why Judah Leib had a dream.

For several years he had been after Mendel Yehudah to buy the St. Laurent abbatoir where he himself was the *kosher* slaughterer, but whenever he asked the rebbe, he replied, "Isn't it enough that you and three other Datschlavers get salaries from St. Laurent and that every year at least ten or more students are away from our people while they learn the art of the ritual slaughter in that *treyfe* environment. The responsibility of a business, we absolutely do not need," the rebbe had always insisted.

But Judah Leib wouldn't give up. He was certain that a slaughterhouse would enable the Datschlavers to enjoy financial independence which they had never had. "We would no longer be dependent on donations," Judah Leib told the rebbe. "The orthodox, Jewish philanthropists always say they have no desire to interfere with our community but they still expect some reward for their generosity. More than once a young Datschlaver had been led astray by those *apikorsim*, and we cannot afford to lose our young men."

As soon as Richard left the *shtiebel*, Judah Leib and Faigele went next door to meet with the rebbe. The rebbetzin greeted them, embracing Faigele warmly. She was particularly fond of the slaughterer's daughter as she was the only other Datschlaver woman who, like herself, had a position of importance in the community.

Judah Leib walked past the two women into the living room. It was almost lunchtime, and he had to be at the St. Laurent abbatoir by two. He scanned the room to see if anyone was waiting. No one. He was in luck.

"Rebbetzin," he called out.

Almost immediately she bustled in from the kitchen with a chrome tray carrying two bowls of piping hot borscht, boiled potatoes swimming in the middle of each, a plate holding six slices of dark rye bread. "Come Judah Leib," she invited.

"You'll have some borscht with the rebbe." Mendel Yehudah usually ate his noon meal alone, pondering the issues presented to him during the morning audiences. Only for especially important meetings did he alter his routine.

The rebbe rose to greet the slaughterer. "Where is Faigele?" he asked. "Rebbetzin, get Faigele and bring her a bowl of borscht. And bring one for yourself, too. The four of us will have lunch together."

Rebbetzin shrugged in amazement as she hurried back to the living room.

"Last night," Rebbe began, when they were seated at the table. "I dreamed we had a fire on Jeanne Mance. Everything burned to the ground, the *shul*, the *yeshiva*, the neighbouring houses. But fortunately, there was not one human casualty. When I woke up at four this morning, I prayed until seven, the time Krakower the beadle usually comes to give me my morning messages and the day's schedule. Krakower reminded me that Richard Vincennes was coming here today. I told him about my dream. 'A sign,' he predicted and he explained why: 'The Gentile came and the Datschlavers were delivered. As the children of Israel were delivered so the Gentile will be the servant. He will lead the Datschlavers to their new home. *Ribonu shel Olam* has led the Datschlavers to Richard Vincennes. And Vincennes has answered the call.'

"Is Krakower correct, Judah Leib? As the good rebbetzin and Faigele are witnesses, have you made a deal with Vincennes? Will we build ourselves a community north of Claremont-Ste Justine?"

Judah Leib chewed his potato, swallowing carefully. At last, he began cautiously. "Richard Vincennes thinks his father will be very interested in our offer. He says two hundred and fifty thousand is extremely generous. He even told me our timing is excellent as recently his parents have spoken about selling their farm and moving to Montreal."

"Indeed, it does sound promising, Judah Leib."

"So far, yes. But you see there is one problem."

"What is it?"

"Well, Richard Vincennes is not returning to Paris. He says he wishes to remain on his parents' farm."

"Exactly like my dream!" declared the rebbe. "But who would believe that a man like Vincennes would live among the Datschlavers? What are you saying, Judah Leib? Faigele, what is your father saying?" the rebbe repeated. "Check your notes and read to me exactly what the Gentile said."

Faigele took her notebook out of her handbag and turned to the pages recording the conversation between Richard Vincennes and her father. She had written down every word: "I would like a home for myself at the edge of your community. Closest to the Laurentians would be my choice. In exchange for this home and a certain lifestyle, I agree to protect the Datschlaver people."

"Protect?" the rebbe interrupted, borscht bubbling out of the corners of his mouth. "A Gentile is going to protect the Datschlavers? To sell us land is one thing but actually to live among us, pursue his own lifestyle? How is such a thing possible? Even *Moshe Rabbenu* didn't enter the promised land. Rebbetzin did you ever hear such foolishness?"

Rebbetzin looked at Faigele, hoping she could provide an explanation. Faigele closed her notebook, afraid to read further.

Rebbe nervously tore a crust from his black bread, shredding it into his soup. "Better finish our borscht," he said, "before it gets cold."

In silence they finished eating and then they sang their blessings. At last, the rebbe spoke. "Faigele, I know I can count on you," he said, as he reached for her notebook. "You are truly a wonder," he continued to praise her. He felt he should because she had no husband and it was necessary for a woman to feel esteemed. Faigele was nineteen and in indeed very marriageable. Rebbe perused her carefully recorded notes. "Enough," he cried out, "I have seen enough. Let's forget the whole deal. What this man asks for is impossible! A *Goy*!" the rebbe bellowed.

But Judah Leib didn't agree. "Please, Rebbe, you should forgive me and *Ribonu shel Olam* should forgive me too if you find what I am about to suggest offensive. But I've been thinking, if we had a business of our own in this new community, maybe Richard Vincennes could help."

"I know you, Judah Leib. You're thinking of that slaughterhouse."

"Why tear down a perfect set-up? Already slaughtering is big business at the Vincennes' farm."

"For the *Goyim*," Rebbe emphasized, but as he spoke, he thought once again of his dream. Maybe the Datschlavers needed this *Goy*, Richard Vincennes.

Judah Leib persisted. "If Vincennes handles the slaughterhouse administration, I can spend more time at my craft and more time with my students. The more I think of it, the more excited I get. Full time at my real vocation."

"What you're suggesting sounds inviting, even possible under the circumstances, but still, we must consider who he is, who we are."

"Exactly. That's why I am recommending Vincennes. Look at his background. An MBA from Harvard Business School, five years with an American multinational company in Paris. Remember, Lou Greisman told you that Vincennes travelled all over the world to sell Harrison, Dunlop and Bloom's farm equipment. Just think what this *Goy* could do with meat."

"I'm telling you, it's not right," Rebbe stroked his beard. He loved the way it felt when he got excited, thick and warm, a touch bristly. He looked at Faigele. It was good to have one woman with hair in the community. And such beautiful hair, he thought to himself. Bowing his head, the rebbe uttered a short prayer, asking forgiveness from *Ribonu shel Olam* for considering for even a minute that Faigele ought to be the only Datschlaver woman forever exempt from shaving her head. Alas, he knew, once married, she too, must obey Datschlaver Law. He thought he would put off finding a match for her so that he might continue to enjoy her black, velvet hair. He added a special prayer for this evil thought, yet, he said, "Faigele, if we do have a slaughterhouse in our new community, your father is going to be a very busy man. I would like you, my dear, to keep on working. For me, and for your father, and I would also like you to assist Mr. Vincennes. Perhaps you can be his secretary too."

"Excuse me, Rebbe," protested Judah Leib. "My daughter cannot be a secretary to this Gentile."

"Rebbetzin," Rebbe asked, "do you think it's all right if our Faigele is a secretary to Mister Vincennes?"

Rebbetzin pulled up the beak of her head scarf. Her bulging eyes which always seemed to pierce people suddenly relaxed. "Our Faigele will be the best secretary Mr. Vincennes has ever had."

"But what about the other Datschlaver women?" Judah Leib asked.

"What about them, Judah Leib? Are they like our Faigele? Faigele is special."

Although Judah Leib thought all his daughters were special, he knew the rebbe had singled out Faigele for a particular destiny. He had always found this puzzling but had never dared to interfere. "Whatever, you say, Rebbe," Judah Leib acknowledged while Faigele also bowed her head in a gesture of obedience.

Rebbe motioned for Judah Leib to rise. Both men spread their prayer shawls over their heads. Soon they were swaying in prayer. Faigele and Rebbetzin, sitting anxiously at the edges of their chairs, opened their *Tehillim* to recite Psalms.

After prayer, Mendel Yehudah reached for his ram's horn, blowing one long, shrill call, before he asked, "Rebbetzin, bring the scotch and four glasses. We will drink to our new community which we shall name after our people. Datschlav. Yes, that's what we shall name it: Datschlav, Quebec."

The Datschlavers were still in excellent financial shape after their purchase of the Vincennes farm. Their bank statement reported assets of close to half a million dollars thanks to donations of philanthropists like Lou Greisman. Rebbe Mendel Yehudah dipped into his people's savings to pay for the move to Datschlav and the rebuilding of the Vincennes farm. The manor and servants' cottage were converted into a temporary synagogue and *yeshiva*, respectively. Small modest dwellings of three and four bedrooms were erected for Datschlaver families. Two ritualaria, one for men and one for women, and separate schools for boys and girls were also built. The pig barn was converted into a garage for maintenance of trucks and tractors, and a general store replaced the horse barn.

Judah Leib personally supervised the conversion of the slaughterhouse. According to Datschlaver injunction, he ordered the *yeshiva* students to carry huge sacks of earth into the building. For several weeks they worked until the rooms were filled halfway to the ceiling, all the cutting and sorting tables, hooks and other instruments of the slaughter completely covered. The doors were bolted, the windows barred. For six months the slaughterhouse remained buried.

Then the day arrived for Judah Leib and Mendel Yehudah to re-open the slaughterhouse in the company of ten of the most pious Datschlavers. For a full week they prayed, morning and evening, before they walked into the building. Brigades of *yeshiva* students were organized to remove earth, scrub walls and floors, hooks and slaughtering instruments until Judah

Leib was satisfied that the laws of purification of buildings and utensils had been carried out.

By the summer Datschlav was complete with thirty-six families from Montreal forming the community. However, *yeshiva* students were still recruited from the four main Datschlaver centres in Montreal, New York, London, and Jerusalem. It was hoped that upon graduation these pious young men would marry wives from home and move to Datschlav to make their family nest.

The first wedding in the community took place two years later, the couple, Faigele Berkovitch and Abe Tarnow. To everyone's surprise the marriage contract stipulated that Faigele would do no housework and that she would continue to be secretary to the rebbe, and Richard Vincennes. Before her marriage Judah Leib had complained bitterly, "Tarnow isn't the right match for Faigele." Having seen that his son Baruch's proposed match drove him from Datschlav, Judah Leib feared for his daughter.

But the rebbe didn't agree with the slaughterer. He had his own reasons for selecting Abe Tarnow which he kept to himself, while he told Judah Leib, "Because Faigele is older than Abe Tarnow and because she has an important job in the community, he will have special respect for her. Faigele will have a good life with Tarnow. Trust my judgment and *Ribonu Shel Olam's*."

The day prior to the wedding, Faigele met with Judah Leib, the rebbe and Richard in the slaughterhouse office above the kill floor. She could hear the stocks opening and closing as every ten minutes an animal's head was locked into position before its throat was slit. She listened to the giant pulley grating along the ceiling as the animals were carried halfway across the room before they dropped with a thud.

What a pity it was that she would soon have to visit the ritual bath. Before immersing in the purification waters, she would have to cut her beautiful black hair, shave her scalp to the quick. The thought made her quite miserable. Still, she was shocked when Rebbe Mendel Yehudah boldly suggested, "I wish Faigele, in your case, we could make an exception. About your hair . . . . Come here, dear, let me stroke it."

Richard wondered whether the rebbe had stroked Faigele's hair on other occasions while Judah Leib kept his eyes riveted on his daughter. Would she comply with the rebbe's request?

Slowly she moved towards him. His bony hand extended from beneath the cape sleeve of his black gaberdine. Tears came to his eyes as he stroked. "I hope, Faigele, you will forgive me but I must touch your hair, this one time."

Faigele tried to smile but she was too nervous. Never had the rebbe or any man touched her hair. "It's a woman's *mitzvah*, Rebbe," she managed to say. "I must carry out the commandment of *Ribonu shel Olam*." Richard sensed her anguish but he remained silent.

Judah Leib and the rebbe covered their heads with their prayershawls. It was time for Richard to leave. The signal was always the same, the bowing of heads, the resumption of prayer.

Richard waited for Faigele at the bottom of the staircase at the side of the building. He knew she would be down in a quarter of an hour, the prescribed time for prayers with Judah Leib and the rebbe after a business meeting, a custom which began after the move to Datschlav. Soon the poor girl would make her way across the boulevard to the women's ritualarium on *Rehov Sara*.

It was five o'clock and the slaughterhouse, though closed for the day, was not yet locked. This was Richard's job, but he deliberately delayed as he paced anxiously back and forth at the bottom of the stairs. "Please come inside," he said firmly to her, when she finally appeared.

"It is not permitted," she replied nervously, but when he held the door open, she quickly stepped inside. The floor had been hosed down, the tables and hooks wiped clean. Except for the smell, there wasn't a sign of the kill. The room appeared very peaceful, Faigele thought. She found herself wishing to prolong her encounter with Richard, to postpone her *mikveh* visit.

Richard had been waiting for this moment for a long time. He reached for Faigele with his strong arms, pressing her tightly against him, before his hands moved directly to her head. "If the rebbe can stroke you, so can I. After all, you're my secretary too. I feel as badly as he does about your hair. Perhaps, worse," he added.

Richard was accustomed to having his way with women, particularly during his five year sojourn in France, so he was surprised when she didn't respond. His hands travelled from her shoulders, down the sides of her shivering arms as he stared hungrily into her eyes.

Faigele truly believed she would be struck dead by *The Holy One Blessed Be He*. She had never been touched affectionately by a man other than her father or brother. Now, within a half hour, two men had stroked her hair. Why was God doing this to her before she shaved her head?

Richard stopped, standing back, as he apologized. "I shouldn't have done that." Walking over to the nearest wall, he pressed his back against it, his hands reaching up for support. Faigele ran out of the slaughterhouse across the boulevard to the women's ritualarium. Richard remained stationed against the wall facing the slaughterhouse door. Any onlooker might have thought he looked like his Lord. But there were no witnesses.

Faigele was due at the *mikveh* at five-thirty. Richard stood frozen in this position until that time.

Faigele Berkovitch and Abe Tarnow were married on August 23rd. Celebrations began after *mincha*, continuing into the early morning hours. Richard, the only Gentile present, sat next to Lou Greisman, who attempted to explain the unusual wedding ritual. Men and women sang songs from their separate tables set up in the open field on the west side of the village beyond the tunnel connecting the men's *yeshiva* to the men's ritualarium.

The pervading colour of the summer annuals, tended with the August wedding in mind, was white. Petunias and alyssum formed a white carpet, except for their tiny yellow centres, green stems, and leaves. Permanent chain link fencing separated men and women. Lou Greisman donated white stephonitis and miniature orchids to dip in and out of the small wire hexagons. A gold satin marriage canopy supported by four posts of birch decorated by climbing sweet pea, again white, stood on a raised dias on the male side of the flowered fence.

The bride did not appear until early evening. At most weddings she is led to the marriage canopy by her father, but in keeping with Datschlaver Law, Faigele walked down the aisle with her closest female relatives, her mother, the good Rebecca Leah, and her three sisters, Sara, Bryna, and Hannah.

The four women wore their usual grey dresses, but for this occasion grey lace trimmed their collars and cuffs. Although their head scarves were also dull grey, they carried open parasols decorated with pink rosebuds and pink ribbons. Hannah, married since she was seventeen, had her little girl, Pennina, a toddler of two and a half, with her.

The child wore a long, pink organza gown with a deeper pink, satin underskirt. She carried a wicker basket filled with rose petals which she tossed along the path as she walked from the rear of the women's section with her mother and aunts. Sara was pregnant for the second time, and Bryna was expecting her first child within a month. Both waddled down the aisle like a pair of misguided ducklings.

Faigele's white satin gown had long sleeves edged with lace extending to tapered points. Tiny seed pearls and sequins trimmed the gown's high collar. She also wore a white silk scarf covered with a lace mantilla tied tightly at the back of her head. Three men sitting in the front row next to Lou Greisman and Richard played their musical instruments, a violin, flute, and viola. Faigele's three sisters and her niece danced, circling the bride, holding their parasols high above her head.

Pennina left their circle and moved close to Faigele, scattering rose petals at her feet.

The actual wedding ceremony was brief, consisting of fifteen minutes of blessings offered by the men while Faigele and her sisters sat on chairs stationed at each of the four posts, supporting the marriage canopy. Pennina sat with the musicians.

Rebbe Mendel Yehudah made an official announcement to the assembled guests. Faigele's marriage provided the perfect occasion for his special gift to her. Secretly he wished it were more. He informed the community that Faigele would continue to lead a different life from other Datschlaver women. Henceforth she would be permitted to study Torah and *Dinim*, the Datschlaver law, the first woman accorded such a privilege. She would do no housework and she would continue to be secretary to her father, the rebbe, and Richard Vincennes.

Mendel Yehudah held up the traditional glass commemorating the destruction of the Temple in Jerusalem. Each of the men in his quorum examined the glass. Hannah, Faigele's sister, displayed the goblet to the women before handing it to Faigele to perform her bridal duty, a duty customarily accorded to the groom. Simon Krakower, totally bewildered with the rebbe's decision, handed a paper bag to Faigele. She put the goblet inside and placed it on the ground. Jumping high in the air, revealing her grey stockinged legs, she landed square on the package, shattering its contents.

The rebbe pronounced Faigele Berkovitch and Abe Tarnow husband and wife. But then he also added, "Faigele will keep her maiden name, *Berkovitch*."

"*Tattenu*," cried each of Faigele's sisters.

"May *The Merciful One* deliver us," sang out Frima, the eldest of the rebbe's daughters, while Pennina jumped up and down, spilling the last of her rose petals on top of the brown bag with the broken glass inside.

The men quickly bowed their heads, praying with renewed fervour. Had Mendel Yehudah gone mad, they wondered.

10

A year and a month from the date of her marriage, Faigele gave birth to a son, Reuben. Simeon was born three years later. Both boys were delivered by Caesarian section, and the doctors advised her that she should not have any more children. At the *yeshiva* the men debated her fate, for a woman did not begin to fulfill the Datschlaver interpretation of the Biblical commandment "Be fruitful and multiply" until she gave birth to eight to ten children.

However, Rebbe Mendel Yehudah unilaterally decreed that many children were not part of Faigele Berkovitch's destiny. On his orders she was to continue her secretarial duties from her home. She was to proceed with her religious studies program. Still, Mendel Yehudah was not satisfied. "I don't see Faigele often enough," he complained to Judah Leib and Richard. "Krakower and Lifsky don't understand me as well as Faigele. I think she should have one of her sisters take care of her children during the day so that she can come to my office to do her work. And Richard, wouldn't you like to have Faigele in the slaughterhouse?"

"I think she should stay home," Richard said, trying to manipulate Mendel Yehudah.

"Where she belongs," added Judah Leib.

When the good women of Datschlav heard that Faigele was no longer staying at home with her children, each had something to say.

Hannah, Faigele's eldest sister, sighed, "Poor Faigele! The Evil Eye shines on her." Bryna, her middle sister, said, "It is not good that a woman should have only two children." Sara chimed in, "If she has only two children, she must have one of each sex."

The rebbetzin's daughters also had their opinions. Frima, the eldest wailed, "O, the sacrilege of Faigele Berkovitch. She has a job!" Shaindel lamented, "She's never home. She works for not one, but two men." Rebecca and Rifkeh cried out together, "Poor Abe Tarnow! The Evil Eye shines on him too!"

But Abe Tarnow didn't care what Faigele did during the day or night. He was a busy man, always rushing around, a bunch of keys swinging from a large brass ring attached to his belt by a piece of soft, brown, braided leather.

Every morning Tarnow left the house at five. He came home at noon for exactly thirty minutes and he did not return again until early evening when he was still in a rush, quickly eating his dinner because of an evening meeting or chores he had not been able to attend to during the day. On weekdays he saw Faigele alone, for an hour at most. On Saturdays he spent most of his time in the synagogue. Saturday evenings he invariably fell asleep at the *melavah malka* celebration bidding farewell to the Sabbath. Sundays, his week began anew.

Abe Tarnow loved the outdoors. Helping Reb Lazare at the train station gave him particular pleasure. When the freight cars with cattle came in from the Abitibi or the Eastern Townships, he would give the signal to unbolt the doors, blowing the whistle which he wore around his neck. He pointed to the slaughterhouse on the right or the barns on the left, and Reb Lazare's students marched the cattle off for either breeding or slaughter. The bulls came from the north and the cows from the south. In Datschlav they met. Abe Tarnow fancied himself a matchmaker of cattle. Three times a week, Monday, Wednesday, and Friday, from eight until ten in the morning he counted and separated animals. Since he was the official male witness, he spent every afternoon at the men's ritualarium. But he also called frequently for unscheduled immersions during the mornings or evenings. He had little time to study Torah and *Dinim*, and as the years passed he

120

began to forget the many passages he had once been able to quote or dispute by rote.

At night when he came home he was always exhausted. He would eat a small snack around ten and then lead Faigele to their bedroom. He was totally ignorant of what it meant to make love to a woman. He never spoke a word nor did he ever see Faigele's body in any decent light. Only with the moon and stars shining through the window did he take in the shadows of her shapely body. Then he performed the act of love quickly, as quickly as he performed all his Datschlav duties.

The months passed and Richard Vincennes became more and more involved in the administration of the slaughterhouse. He had less time for his family and friends both in Claremont-Ste Justine and Montreal. In awe as he had once been of the Hasidim, their austere life and strict rituals began to irritate him. However, his admiration for the slaughterer and his daughter continued to grow as he sensed they were the only Datschlavers who were dissatisfied with the community status quo, except for the renegade son, Baruch, whom no one spoke of anymore.

Grateful for his personal attention, Judah Leib and Faigele made Richard feel extraordinarily special. Indeed, he represented a foreign world whose knowledge they were desperately eager to have and he alone had the power to impart. Secretly, Richard set up a library for the slaughterer and his daughter behind a false panel in the wall of Judah Leib's study. In front of the wall were Judah Leib's Datschlaver books: *Dinim* and *Dinim* commentary, the Bible, prayerbooks, and the Babylonian and Jerusalem editions of Talmud. Next to Mendel Yehudah, Judah Leib was the most accomplished scholar in Datschlav but he had very little worldly knowledge.

Richard arranged for Judah Leib to visit the Jewish Public Library. There were so many books that he had not read, and secular Judaica seemed like a safe place to start. One morning at five-thirty the security guard at the library opened the back door for the Datschlaver. Accompanied by Richard, Judah Leib toured room after room. He conducted a random check. If he read a title which raised his curiosity, he opened the book and began a short skim. Then, shaking his head in disapproval, he offered a quick prayer, asking forgiveness from *The Holy One Blessed Be He*.

Richard thought he had made a terrible blunder bringing Judah Leib to the library when the slaughterer suddenly announced: "Get a master list. We'll borrow everything."

"Even the books you disapprove of?" Richard asked.

"Even those," answered Judah Leib. "I'll read them all."

"We can't take all these books. Not at once. This is a public library. I'll make a selection with the librarian. When you finish a few, we can get more."

"Don't you go telling the librarian I've never read a secular Jewish book," Judah Leib said. But soon, the slaughterer chuckled, "I don't want anyone in Datschlav to know I'm reading and I don't want anyone outside Datschlav to know I'm not."

"This is a problem for your sages," Richard concluded.

Now they both laughed. The security guard who overheard their conversation laughed too.

Several volumes of Jewish history were delivered to Datschlav. Judah Leib couldn't decide which book to read first. Richard suggested two volumes of Josephus and an archeological study of the Middle East during the Biblical period. Soon the slaughterer was reading several interpretations of the controversy between the Sadducees and the Pharisees. He found it hard to believe that none of the authors were rabbis. He was particularly interested in the plight of the Jews during the Spanish Inquisition, the Marranos who converted to Christianity to save their lives and then secretly practised Judaism. He read Maimonides' *Guide to the Perplexed* and Spinoza's *Ethics* and even the writings of other Hasidic rebbes. For the first time in his life, he began to grasp how unique and different the Datschlavers were.

Richard encouraged Faigele to share her father's newly discovered pleasure. She read as much as Judah Leib, but while her father began to feel guilty about his deception, she savoured the excitement and danger. She longed to know the man who made so many wonderful books available to her and her father.

One day in Judah Leib's office at the slaughterhouse, Faigele got up the courage to ask, "Richard, if I visit your home, can I see your books?"

"What if someone sees you?"

"What if someone does?" she said with stubborn defiance, adjusting her head scarf. Her eagerness delighted him. "You do what you like, Faigele Berkovitch."

11

"You do what you like, Faigele Berkovitch." What pleasure those words gave. She kept turning them over in her mind after he said them. No Datschlaver ever did what he or she liked, only what was prescribed day after day.

A month later she decided to visit Richard at his home. How she fussed over her preparations, even though attention to one's physical appearance was forbidden, except for one's husband and then only prior to the Sabbath and other holidays. After visiting the ritual bath, Datschlaver wives were given short wigs to wear from sundown to sunset. The women removed their headscarves so the rebbetzin could match their shorn heads with the right colour wig. For this purpose each woman had a tuft of hair, a perfect triangle at the base of her scalp. Rebbetzin admonished anyone who complained that her clump was a different colour than her selected holiday wig. "The Evil Eye deceives you."

Faigele brooded. How she wished she could rip that hideous patch from her head. To diminish the thought of its ugliness she chose a deep red scarf dotted with pink roses on thin, olive green stems. She wore her most attractive grey dress, one with lace trimming its high collar. What vanity she scolded herself as she hastened to the cold storage room next to her kitchen to uncover the only mirror in the house on the back of the utility room door. She quickly tore off the sheet and carefully began the finishing touches, tightening her waistband, wishing she had a colourful cummerbund to break up all the grey, smoothing her full dress over her hips and tying her scarf at the back of her head. Her heart beat so wildly she thought she would truly die. She rushed out of her house through the back door of the utility room, hoping no one would see her.

The snow fell in large scales. A wet snow. When she reached Richard's home, her head scarf was soaking. She took off her grey gloves and rummaged in her purse. In her excitement she had forgotten to consider the weather. "No scarf," she fretted, as she waited at the side door. She was about to turn away when Richard greeter her.

"Where are you going, Faigele Berkovitch?"

Panic stricken she slipped inside the open door. At that very moment she had seen her sisters wheeling their prams past Richard Vincennes' residence.

"Isn't that Faigele?" said Sara.

"*Tattenu*, is it possible?" replied Hannah.

"Look at the door. It's Mr. Vincennes," said Bryna. "What's he doing home in the middle of the day?"

"Faigele usually sees him in his office at the slaughterhouse. Why is she seeing him at home, I wonder?" The other sisters shrugged, bending to adjust their sleeping infants' blankets.

"Maybe she's got business," Bryna said.

Hannah sighed, "Some business!"

"She's wearing her *yontif* coat!" exclaimed Sara.

"A-a-a-a-h," they sang, "The Evil Eye shines on her, a-a-a-h . . . " They moved on, pushing their prams quickly, their grey coats opening to the wind.

Faigele realized she had been spotted. Embarrassed and horrified, her face reddened while her eyes filled with tears.

"You'd best take off that wet scarf and wrap this towel around your head," Richard said.

Faigele yielded, succumbing easily to his calm demand.

"There's a mirror on the back of the pantry door," Richard said.

Faigele had never seen such a mirror. In contrast, her own proved dim, its reflection even deceiving. Only the mirror in the synagogue could match Richard's.

Faigele marvelled at her image. She had never realized how slim her waist looked. Her figure was positively alluring, except for the towel on her head, heavy and cumbersome, reminding her of who she was. What if Richard were to see that hideous tuft? She wanted to sneak out before it was too late. Once more, she turned to leave.

"You're not going anywhere!" he said. "Gregoire, my butler, will see that your scarf is dry and ironed in a few moments."

"I'll wait in the back hall," Faigele stammered, "until my scarf is ready."

"I almost forgot," Richard smiled, touching her shoulder gently. "I have a present for you." He reached into the pantry cupboard, taking out a large white and black hatbox, secured with a redolent rose.

"Don't just stand there. Open your gift," Richard encouraged.

He removed the rose and handed her the hatbox. "You are a bud, tender and sweet, more beautiful than this rose," he said softly, studying her face while he spoke.

Never had Tarnow spoken such words. Never had he stared at her in this manner, nor had he ever touched her as gently. Occasionally he gave her fingertips a light squeeze, almost like an alternate form of handshake, but immediately after he would hasten to put a coin in the charity collection box, to ask forgiveness from *The Holy One Blessed Be He.*

Slowly Faigele opened the hatbox. Richard had retired to the main drawing room while she thought about running away, until she saw what was inside. A wig! As close in colour to her own real hair as she could remember. It had been five years since her hair was long and thick, falling all the way down to her hips. The wig felt warm and protective. She began to scorn her shaved head and the cruel Datschlaver custom.

Looking at her reflection in the mirror she saw only anger in her eyes. She didn't want to think about her people, the rebbe, or the rebbetzin, or even her own family. She felt wildly unrestrained. She opened the pantry door which led to an enormous kitchen painted soft beige with a cantilevered oak ceiling supporting copper pots. Dozens of knives, spatulas, wooden spoons, and wire whisks were lined up along the counter top near the stove. A stove with two ovens and shining glass doors. Through the casement windows trimmed with burnt orange ruffle, Faigele saw the sun breaking through the snow clouds, catching the surfaces of the shining pots and pans. The smell of cooking fish filled the room. An oversized pepper mill stood on the chopping board close to the stove. Racks of spices were lined up against a wall behind the stove. Never had Faigele seen such a kitchen.

Richard returned, having changed from a tweed suit into a pair of grey flannels and a widely ribbed turtle neck sweater. He smoked a meerschaum pipe with a king's head carved on the bowl. He appeared so content, Faigele thought, as he smiled, taking the pipe from his lips. "And how is the fair Faigele?" he asked. "Well, speak up, do you like your gift?"

"Do I like it? I love it!" she finally answered. Gently, he took her in his arms and she imagined many young Datschlaver women like herself with long wigs dancing in a protective circle around her and Richard. She wanted to leave their circle until he pressed urgently against her, pulling her into his very being. "This is foolish," he said. Nevertheless, he tucked her hand firmly in his, confidently leading her through the front hall.

In the main drawing room heavy burgundy velvet drapes hung from the wooden valences above two sets of double casement windows covered by batiste sheers, the side drapes pulled back by pink satin cord braiding. At the far end of the room bevelled glass doors, trimmed with cherrywood matching the hall panelling, closed off yet another drawing room. Because the doors were open, Faigele saw a fireplace flanked by ceiling to floor bookcases. Two burgundy velvet-covered wing chairs stood in front of the fireplace. Her attention was drawn not to the furniture, the soft velvet upholstered chairs and sofas or the black, lacquered tables with colourful marble inlay, but to the walls with their paintings.

Three of the canvasses celebrated the female nude. She covered her eyes as soon as she saw them. Still, Richard seem oblivious to her shyness about art as he proceeded to lecture her. "They may not be masters like Ingres or Renoir," he explained, "but, they are classical gems. Unfortunately the artist, Froebell, is an unknown. A shame, because he's so good. I'm very fond of his work. He was born in Germany but he moved to France in the early 1870s. He was influenced by Pierre Auguste Renoir, famous for his paintings of the female nude."

Faigele winced for she had virtually no understanding of the human body as art belonging to man rather than *The Holy One Blessed Be He.*

Richard continued, "Renoir's women are always plump. Never a crease in the skin." Faigele smiled weakly, as he elaborated. " 'A tight fit, like an animal's coat,' one critic described it. Come my Faigele, take your hands from your eyes and enjoy. Here, notice Froebell's women's spontaneity of gesture. Sadly, the man died at the age of twenty-seven of a rare bone disease. They say over two-hundred women posed naked for him."

Faigele was preoccupied, studying one of the paintings. A fat woman admired her naked image in a full-length mirror. Her pendulous breasts hung loosely but her broad hips were firm and shiny as marble. The woman resembled Rebbetzin.

"What's the matter?" said Richard. "Are you upset?"

"I don't care for this one," said Faigele, not telling Richard why the painting made her anxious. She thought about her brother. Maybe he, too, painted naked women.

"You're thinking about Baruch, aren't you?"

"Yes. How did you know?"

"I guessed. *L'enfant terrible.*" Richard paused. "How did your people get so crazy?" he asked.

Faigele did not answer. She continued studying the adjacent two paintings: *L'homme prisonnier* and *Julie et L'Universe.* The first painting of a prisoner's back in irreconcilable tones of black and white reminded her of her brother when he lived in Datschlav. The second painting also moved her: a solitary figure floating in a winter scene, a woman taking on the stillness of the snow around her.

Once again Richard lectured Faigele. "Jean Paul Lemieux, born in 1904. He is known for his stylized portraiture, his strong sentiment. He'd be pleased to get a hold of a few Datschlavers to paint. Your people would fascinate him. Why are you so silent, Faigele?"

"I am not supposed to look at these pictures."

"I will be your eyes, your painter if you will. You are lovely, like the woman in the painting. See, Faigele, how she walks off the page."

Richard led Faigele to his study. He sat down on one of the burgundy wing chairs, pulling her gently on to his lap. He looked into her eyes, drawing small circles on her forehead with his fingertips. He undid the buttons of her grey cotton dress. When he tried to make love to her on the thick white carpet, she panicked and froze. "If you don't stop acting like a stuck pig," he said coldly, "I'll have to spank you."

Why, thought Faigele. What have I done wrong? Yet, she knew she was guilty and that she should not be here. The image of the pig sickened her. She was impure like the ai her people were forbidden to eat. Richard pulled her to feet, forced her to sit with him on the wing chair, recline acro his knees, her back arched uncomfortably, her neck raised like a swan's. "Why are you here, Faigele?" he muttered as he entered her again, grunting deeply with his pleasure when he finished.

Like a pig, she kept thinking as he caressed her buttocks. "Sweet Faigele, will you forgive me," he whispered, pulling her to the floor. She wept quietly as he began to make love to her again, but this time she willingly surrendered.

Richard brewed tea for Faigele. Usually Gregoire served afternoon tea but Richard had dismissed him, not wanting to spoil his intimacy with Faigele.

Never before had a man prepared tea for her. And never in such splendid china, cups and saucers with hand-painted flowers, a gleaming silver spoon with which to stir in the sugar. She could actually see her reflection shining in the bowl of the spoon.

"I have another gift for you," he announced, leading her to the bookshelves. He fingered the spines of two or three books before he reached for *The Tin Flute* by Gabrielle Roy. "I have the book in French too but I think you will find the English easier." Faigele and the rebbetzin were the only women in Datschlav who knew how to speak and read French. Richard showed Faigele the French edition. She read the title and smiled, "*Bonheur d'occasion*. You are my secondhand happiness, Richard." Faigele pressed the novel to her breast. "The author of this book is a woman?" she said.

"Of course, see for yourself. *Gabrielle Roy*. Her name is on the book's spine and here on the title page."

"A woman writes a book. That's really something. We have only a few female sages in Jewish history. Deborah, the Judge, and Berurya, the wife of Rabbi Meir. But neither of these women recorded their thoughts. They were recorded for them by men."

"Faigele, that was thousands of years ago. It's different today, even for orthodox Jewish women."

Faigele did not appear to hear him as she continued. "Mendel Yehudah wants me to be like Berurya but I don't have the time to devote to my studies." Suddenly, Faigele was overcome by a deep gloom, an all encompassing sadness. She bit her lip. "*Niddah*," she said, her fists clenched, "I hate *niddah* . . . "

Richard wiped her lips with his handkerchief and kissed her softly. Faigele tensed. "I must leave now," she said, "what shall I do with the wig?"

"Leave it here until next time. I need you, Faigele." He held both her hands tightly, brushing her fingers with his lips.

Faigele's troubled eyes still did not clear. "Is my scarf in the kitchen?" she asked.

"Gregoire left it in the back hall. I have a special shelf for your wig. Come, I'll show you."

"Do you want to tell me about *niddah*?" Richard asked as he led Faigele through the kitchen to the back hallway.

"I can't speak to you about *niddah*. It's not permitted."

"But Faigele . . . "

"I have already broken the Law by coming here . . . I have let you make love to me." She paused. "And the wig, I have so enjoyed the wig." She reached to take it off. "Please could you turn around while I do this?"

On the shelf stood a mannequin's upper torso and head, the face featureless. When Faigele took off her wig and placed it on the figure, she felt like they were trading places.

12

"Where were you for the children's supper?" her sister, Hannah asked as soon as she walked through the front door.

"Where was Mama?" four-year-old Reuben echoed his aunt.

"Mama was with Mr. Vincennes," Faigele told Hannah and her little boy. Simeon, the baby, banged his spoon on his plate. "Stop that," Faigele snapped. Alarmed, he started to cry.

"See what you've done," Hannah said. "You've upset the baby."

"I'm sorry," Faigele said, "I'm tired." She walked over to the kitchen table and lifted the child out of his high chair, cuddling him in her arms.

"Tired are you?" said Hannah. "What were you doing then for so long at Mister Vincennes'? Sara, Bryna and I saw you go into the house at three o'clock."

Faigele glanced at her watch. Ten past six. Had she been at Richard's for three hours. She had meant to stay only a half hour. She checked to make certain her head scarf was properly adjusted. As she felt the flimsiness of the soft silk, she thought of the warmth of the wig she had recently worn. A rush of memories of the few hours with Richard flowed through her mind and she could hardly hear what her sister said. I'll have to go to the *mikveh*, she thought to herself. How will I explain to Hannah?

Since her sister was the official female witness at the ritualarium, she had to be summoned every time an immersion took place. Like Abe Tarnow, Faigele's husband, Hannah always carried a set of keys, but unlike him she could only be

131

called in the hours after sunset and before dawn to perform her official duties of observation.

Faigele asked hesitantly, "Hannah, could you supervise an immersion for me this evening?"

"I had you at the *mikveh* less than a week ago," Hannah answered perfunctorily. She knew every woman's menstrual cycle by heart, including the irregularities, as she kept track of both in a black book beside her set of keys in her apron pocket. She immediately consulted her records to make certain she was not mistaken. "Yes," she confirmed, "four days ago you were ready to *don the white.*" This meant that Faigele had immersed as prescribed seven days after the termination of her menses and was therefore officially declared ready to resume sexual relations with her husband. "Staining?" her sister wasted no time in asking. "Yes," mumbled Faigele, seizing the opportunity to use the monstrous set of regulations to her own advantage. She wouldn't feel right sleeping with Tarnow if she did not go to the *mikveh* after making love with Richard. This was to be her own privately tailored *niddah* law and she was pleased to have thought of it. With her usual confidence and air of superiority, she informed her sister of only what she expected to hear. "Two days ago, I began staining. I performed *bedikah* for two evenings. Yesterday morning I was still staining but today I was clean."

"Are you certain?" Hannah asked. "If you've saved your *bedikah* cloth, I can show it to Peretz."

"It is not necessary, Hannah. I am quite certain of my cleanliness. Absolutely, no question about my readiness to *don the white,*" she said, scornfully. She loathed the idiotic expression almost as much as the custom itself. Being preoccupied with the minute detail of her menstrual cycle repelled her. Still, she continued to play the game with Hannah, to give her the assurance she required. "I've already laundered my *bedikah* cloth," she safely added.

"That's good," said Hannah. "Today especially, Peretz is so busy. Last week nine women had *shaalohs*, every day, including the weekend when five more started to ask. Come the beginning of this week and Peretz still had nine from the previous week. Every day, all these women staining. That's fourteen of them performing *bedikah* nightly, and poor Peretz having to check all fourteen. Sometimes, he can't be certain on his own and he must consult Mendel Yehudah. To tell you the truth, it takes so much time, he resents it. I tell him I could help; after all, who gives him the cloths? I could save them, bring them all to him at one time. The women are not on a schedule like the men; the cloths come in between seven and ten in the morning. No sooner does Peretz go off to *yeshiva*, he has to return to his office at the women's ritualarium to check another *bedikah* cloth. He likes each one should be fresh," she hesitated to add. "Why keep the women waiting?"

"As *dayan*, it's his job," Faigele reminded. "He shouldn't resent it." She was desperately trying to sidetrack her sister from her own situation. She could see it was working. Hannah, a very nervous woman, was now totally on the defensive for having suggested that her husband might be balking a Datschlaver custom. "Peretz is a good Datschlaver," her sister announced.

"Did I say he wasn't good? Only he should carry out his job with love and respect. He should rush back with sheer pleasure from the *yeshiva* to check those cloths. Does he wear gloves?" Faigele asked, taking the opportunity to pry further into Peretz's *bedikah* routine.

"Of course, he wears gloves," said Hannah. "And he is very thorough. When he cannot be certain on his own, in the case of yellow staining, he checks for the slightest tinge of red or brown with a magnifying glass before he bothers Mendel Yehudah with a *shaaloh*. Peretz is meticulous when it comes to *bedikah*," said Hannah.

"So am I," smiled Faigele, regaining her composure. "After I put the children to bed, you will come with me to the *mikveh*. That will give you time to go home and give your children dinner. If you hurry, I can be back in time to study some *Dinim* before Tarnow comes home. On days when I visit Mr. Vincennes, he has dinner at Mendel Yehudah's."

"Mendel Yehudah knows you visit Mr. Vincennes?"

"He knew I was going to his home today, if that's what you are getting at?"

"But usually you see him at your office above the slaughterhouse, don't you?"

"Usually," answered Faigele, but today I was invited to his home. Mendel Yehudah, himself, gave me permission to go."

"I see," said Hannah. "Who am I to question the rebbe, yet I'll have you know, I don't like it. Mr. Vincennes is supposed to live apart from us. Start visiting him at his home and you're asking for trouble. The Evil Eye," her sister warned.

"I'm not afraid of The Evil Eye," Faigele said. "And I think you're foolish to have mentioned it. You may live in constant fear of demons but I don't. I do what I like."

"She does what she likes!" her sister repeated as she busied herself with cleaning up the dishes, wiping the table and sweeping the floor. Faigele went into the living room with the children. She played with them while she waited for her sister to leave, but Hannah was obviously taking her time with her chores. Faigele sensed her sister would have more to say about her visit to Richard's house, but she surprised her, giving her usual silent bow as a show of respect before she left and also saying that she would meet Faigele at the *mikveh* in an hour.

Faigele smiled condescendingly at her. She had earned this right to be different and she always took her authority very seriously. To keep everyone in awe of those who were in charge was absolutely necessary. This she had learned as soon as the community moved to Datschlav, but then it had always been this way, only more so since the move from Montreal.

"Mama, what's *bedikah*?" Reuben asked as soon as his Aunt Hannah was out of ear shot.

"A check-up," Faigele quietly explained.

"What do you mean, a check-up?" the child inquired further. He was always asking questions. A prodigy, he was already reading the Bible and he knew vast sections by heart.

"When you try to find out if something is the way it should be," Faigele told him.

"Are you the way you should be, Mama?"

"Of course, I am, Darling."

"Then, why do you work every day while all the other mothers stay home? Why do you work for the rebbe and Mr. Vincennes? I've even seen you talking to them. Aunt Hannah never talks to them and Aunt Bryna and Aunt Sara don't talk to them either."

"Reuben, I am different from my sisters because Rebbe Mendel Yehudah wants me to be different. He has chosen me to do special work in Datschlav. Work that will help everyone who lives in our community."

"I don't care about everyone else. I wish you were here all day, instead of my aunties. I like them but I like you better."

Tears welled up in Faigele's eyes. She herself didn't fully understand how she had come to have a different destiny from her fellow Datschlaver women. As far back as she could remember, the rebbe had singled her out. First in primary school when she was the only child who took French. When she turned sixteen, Mendel Yehudah decided that she should accompany her father to the Montreal slaughterhouses. He insisted that she abandon her black oxfords when she travelled with Judah Leib. "You must look modern, my Faigele, when you go outside the community. Those oxfords don't do much for you," he had added, carefully weighing his words. The rebbe to this day selected her footwear, high heeled laced boots, grey soft leather in winter and white shining vinyl in summer. The boots reached up past the hem of her long dress, all the way up to her knees. From time to time Mendel Yehudah would ask Faigele to lift her skirt to her mid-calf so that he could see how her boots fit. Faigele sensed the look on his face indicated that he was admiring her slender calves, though he never admitted it. Now, having been with Richard in his home, having had a man verbally praise every part of her body, she suspected the rebbe may have had something else on his mind.

And Richard had given her a gift, the most precious gift possible, a wig. Never before had Faigele received a gift of such a personal nature. And a gift to be enjoyed in Richard's presence alone, a gift that would be shunned by her people, if they knew about it. She had also let Richard make love to her, say and do passionate, wild things. Forbidden things, she had never done before.

She looked thoughtfully at Reuben. She could tell he wanted her to say more. She tried to concentrate on what was important to say to the child. "The rebbe has encouraged me to work and study for the sake of our people," she explained. "You know Mama studies every night from *Dinim*. You know the rebbe asks me every day how many pages I have learned. Tonight after you go to sleep, I will learn three new sections and tomorrow the rebbe will ask me about what I have studied."

"What will Mr. Vincennes ask you?" the child piped up.

"He's going to Montreal tomorrow," Faigele replied in order to satisfy her son's insatiable curiosity.

"Are you going with him?"

"No, son."

"I'm glad," said Reuben. "If you're not with me, I don't want you to be with him."

"Reuben, you should not speak disrespectfully. When I go to Montreal with Mister Vincennes, we visit many of the butcher shops to arrange for the shipment of Datschlav's meat. We also pick up supplies that everyone needs."

"You're always talking about everyone but Aunt Hannah told me where you were today. You were at *his* house. All alone with *him*. Aunt Hannah says The Evil Eye got hold of you. Is it true, Mama? Will the Evil Eye get me too?"

"Aunt Hannah is always afraid. Don't pay attention to what she tells you about The Evil Eye. Now, come along and help me put Simeon to bed. Then you'll say your prayers, like a good boy. And no more questions tonight, okay."

"Yes, Mama."

After both the children were in bed, Faigele went to her bedroom to get a few belongings together to take to the *mikveh*. She always used her own towel and wash cloth as she disliked the thin worn out towels supplied at the ritualarium. She also took her own scented soap, expensive perfume and body lotion, items she purchased during her trips to Montreal with her father and Richard, luxuries shunned in the community. Why was she going to the *mikveh*? she asked herself as she packed the few items. Had the immersion habit been so entrenched that she treated Richard as a symbol of defilement? Her initial pride in deciding to go to the *mikveh* suddenly repelled her. She called Hannah on the phone to say she would not be going to the *mikveh*, after all. Her sister was shocked as Faigele had told her earlier that she had been staining, but now was clean. The *niddah* law was clear, requiring her sister to visit the *mikveh*. Faigele, however, did not waiver from her invented story. Asserting even more initiative, she told her sister: "I have been given dispensation by Mendel Yehudah. You see, Hannah, I didn't give you all the facts. Not that you didn't question me thoroughly . . . it was hardly your fault." She wanted her sister to feel guilty but she got no reaction from Hannah. Still she persisted. "This morning I took my *bedikah* cloth to Mendel Yehudah. The rebbe told me he thought I was clean but he wasn't sure. He called me this evening just after you left the house to say that he had reconsidered and that I am not ready to *don the white*."

"I see," said Hannah, obviously flustered. "Mendel Yehudah before my Peretz. Shall I tell him, Faigele?"

"Absolutely not," said Faigele boldly. "I shall inform Peretz myself. I have decided I will never again give my *bedikah* cloths to your husband. After all, I am Faigele Berkovitch," she proclaimed to her astonished sister, before changing the subject. "Tomorrow, I shall bring Reuben and Simeon to your place at eight-thirty. I have to be at the rebbe's by nine for my

Dinim lesson. I must be on time because Mister Vincennes will be in Montreal and I need to report to the slaughterhouse by ten."

"I'll be expecting you at eight-thirty," Hannah said cordially.

"Thank you, Hannah. Good Night."

The next morning when Faigele entered the rebbe's office he was already poring over the three pages of *Dinim* concerning the sabbatical year. Since it was seven years since the inception of Datschlav, particularly the restoration of the slaughterhouse and the cultivation of the fields for the cattle that would eventually go to slaughter, the rebbe wished to discuss with Faigele the feasibility of closing down the abbatoir for a year. He always interpreted the law in such a way that it could have direct bearing on the Datschlavers' contemporary situation. He respected Faigele's opinion on such matters. She had practical insights he could not always see. A woman's mind. Why he no longer called upon the rebbetzin for such interpretation was now widely accepted. Ever since Faigele had turned sixteen, he had made it a practise to consult his wife less and less. It was all part of his plan for Faigele. But no sooner had they begun to discuss the sabbatical year than the rebbe started to yawn.

"I see you are tired," Faigele said. "You must not have slept well last night."

"All night I had strange dreams," he admitted. "Dreams about you, my Faigele, and Richard Vincennes. I couldn't believe what the Faigele in my dreams did," the rebbe continued, before confronting her. "I know you were at Richard's for three hours yesterday. I had thought you would be quick about the visit. Remember, I told you, only a half hour, at suppertime. Why did you disobey me, go early, and stay for three hours?"

Faigele blanched with fear and fell to her knees. Frantically she began kissing the edges of the rebbe's caftan. "I'm sorry I stayed so long. Please don't find displeasure with me." She began to weep and wail, like the other Datschlaver women.

Mendel Yehudah put his hands on her shoulders, gently stroking them. "Do not be frightened, my Faigele. I am your rebbe. I am also your friend. You must tell me everything that happened between you and Mister Vincennes. I will understand."

Faigele stood slowly as the rebbe helped her to her feet. He was so close that she could feel his hot breath on her cheeks while he stared directly into her eyes. For the first time she realized that although his hair was grey as was his beard, his eyes still looked youthful. He had very clear, hazel eyes and he looked at her now with a bold sense of lustful adventure.

"Pick up your skirt, Faigele," he whispered as he moved away. "I need to see how your boots fit."

She did as he requested. Her soft grey leather boots were laced tightly around her slender ankles and calves. Usually, Rebbe bade her expose her boots only up to her mid-calf, but today he said, "Lift your dress further, my Faigele, to the very top of your boots. I've been worried lately about how tightly laced they are. I must examine your flesh to see if it's free enough for adequate blood circulation. It will be hard for me to ascertain through your black stockings but I'm determined to check very carefully." The rebbe sat down in his chair and bade Faigele approach. He stared at her knees as she stood before him. Reaching his hands behind, he drew them forward to his waiting, parted lips, pressing his wet mouth against her black stockings. She squealed with pleasure as his open lips traced a path from her knees to her bare thighs. She wanted him to kiss her flesh. "More, more," she cried out. He bit the inside of her upper thigh, his tongue touching the edge of her cotton panties. She grasped his earlocks, twisting them in her hands, rubbing them against his face. She could no longer bear the bliss and mortification. Faigele Berkovitch lost consciousness.

When she awoke, her garters were in place, her stockings straight. Only her damp panties reminded her of what had happened. The rebbe sat at his desk poring over the *Dinim* passage they were to discuss. When he beckoned Faigele to take her usual seat, she cringed with fear. Not until the end of the discussion concerning the sabbatical year did the rebbe refer to what happened earlier. "Faigele," he said calmly, with his usual authority, "you must speak to me about your visits with Mr. Vincennes. You must be completely open," he continued. "Tell me whatever happens between you. I need to know everything," he said, smiling. "Do you understand?"

"Yes, Rebbe."

"And now, my Faigele, I give you my permission to visit Mister Vincennes as often as you like."

"You do, Rebbe."

"Yes, Faigele, I do."

Faigele made her way from rebbe's home across the Boulevard *Rehov Zion* to the slaughterhouse. It was after ten when she arrived. Her father waited, sitting in Richard's office next to hers. Usually he didn't leave the kill floor during the day, but this morning because of the absence of Richard and his daughter, he had to attend to some administrative matters until Faigele arrived. He looked up from his bills and other correspondence when he heard his daughter's voice. "Hello, Papa. How are you this morning?"

"Not too well, Faigele, not too well," he said.

She saw that he was wearing an amulet to ward off The Evil Eye. It was silver, and it hung from his neck by a blue ribbon. In the centre was a tree of life, over which was depicted the image of a woman with long dark hair and wings. On the bottom of the amulet was inscribed *keyn ayen hore*, may there be no Evil Eye, and the name of the she-demon herself, Lilith. "What's wrong, Papa?" she asked. "Why are you afraid that Lilith is about?"

"It's not me who is afraid. It is your mother and your sisters. They wouldn't let me come to the slaughterhouse today without this amulet. Faigele, your sisters saw you going into Richard Vincennes' house yesterday. They fear that you are

140

possessed by The Evil Eye, maybe even Lilith herself, and they warned me to keep my distance lest The Evil Eye get hold of me too."

"Oh, Papa, I'm tired of their idiotic superstitions, aren't you? I had quite a time with Hannah yesterday afternoon when I returned from Richard's. Even Reuben questioned me. I can't stand their meddling. Have they no respect?"

"They do respect you, my dear, but that doesn't mean they cannot be afraid. They value us and they do not want to see us possessed by demons. I can understand how they feel, even though I, like you, no longer believe in such things. One has to accommodate the people with whom one lives. For *shalom bayit*, no? Come close, my dear, and let me put some of this blue paint on your forehead. That's better," he said, as he painted an open hand in between her two eyebrows, the thumb pointing to one side. "Now you yourself are trying to get rid of what possesses you," he explained.

"Possesses me. Why? What have I done wrong."

"You visited Richard Vincennes at his home for three hours. The women who are closest to you, your mother and your sisters, are convinced the man has seduced you. Your mother didn't mince any words when she confronted me. You see, Hannah told her your story concerning your desire to go to the *mikveh*. First you wanted to go, then you didn't. Hannah thought you acted most peculiar. She told your mother and your sisters and together they decided that you must be a fallen woman, possessed The Evil Eye, maybe even Lilith herself. They have asked me to prevail upon you to visit the *mikveh* before it is too late. They are waiting for you there."

"I absolutely refuse," Faigele shouted. "It's barbaric."

"Faigele, even if it is barbaric, it satisfies them and keeps them quiet. In Datschlav, *shalom bayit* means peace in the entire community. Go my child and get the *mikveh* over with."

"If you really think I must."

"I do. I'll stay here until you get back."

"Papa, do you think I did wrong, visiting Richard at his home?"

"Faigele, you see him in my private study and you see him here. I hardly think it necessary for you to go to his home."

Faigele nodded. "Perhaps you are right. But he invited me and I didn't think a short visit would do any harm."

Her father looked back at the paper work in front of him. He fingered the amulet hanging from his neck. "I have nothing more to say," he said. "Just go to the *mikveh* as you've been told to do."

With a stern look on her face she turned and hurried out of the office, determined to get this silliness over with as quickly as possible. She walked back across the Boulevard *Rehov Zion*, this time in the direction of the women's *mikveh*. Her sisters and her mother waited for her at the door, amulets identical to her father's hanging from their necks. They had their arms clasped about each others' waists and they formed a barrier so that she could not pass. She nodded formally to all of them. "So, here I am, the she-demon herself, coming to be cleansed. I assume that's what you're after."

Rebeccah Leah screamed when Faigele said this. Her daughters cried out, "Don't frighten Mother, you she-demon, you."

"Don't you want me to take my clothes off?" Faigele asked.

Her mother turned around. "Absolutely not. You could taint the waters with your private parts." Then her scorn turned into wailing as she led her daughters, the impure one and the pure to the ritual bath. As soon as they were inside the room, she bade her impure daughter be seated for a glass of sweet wine. "Wine before the *mikveh*?" asked Faigele.

"When warding off The Evil Eye," her mother explained, "or grappling with someone who is likely possessed by the she-demon herself, we need to make sure the suspect is relaxed. The procedure in each case must be innovative. For you, since you visited Mister Vincennes for three hours at his home, we must summon the most unusual of routines at our disposal.

142

Sip, my daughter, and may the monster that possesses you slip from your body."

Rebeccah Leah urged Faigele to drink two more full cups of wine after the first, one for each hour she had visited with Richard.

Faigele began to relax and feel groggy. She felt her eyelids grow heavy and soon she could hardly keep her eyes open. But she was certain, as she stared dimly ahead, that her mother was removing her headscarf and she appeared to be placing small patches of hair on her head. Did she know about the wig, Faigele wondered?

Faigele didn't realize that the small patches of hair were leeches. Having consulted an obscurantist text for the exorcising of a demon that might have lured Faigele to Mr. Vincennes' home for three hours, the women discovered that only leeches would suffice. They would suck at the victim's scalp as she was immersed in the ritual bath, and the wicked *jinn* would leave her body. Her mother led her fully clothed into the pool. The leeches clung to her bare head while she dipped the prescribed three times. Her sisters watched from the edge of the water, each one with her left thumb in her right hand and her right thumb in her left hand, while her mother at her side made sure none of the leeches fell off. The sisters recited, "We the devoted siblings of Faigele Berkovitch, are legitimate heirs of Joseph whom The Evil Eye may not affect." As soon as they said this, Rebeccah Leah took one of the leeches from Faigele's head and placed it between the eyebrows of her daughter, on the blue paint her father had marked on her forehead. But the leeches kept falling off when Faigele dipped below the water's surface, and Rebeccah Leah had to keep putting them back on. After she led her daughter out of the pool, she removed the leeches. Faigele's sisters dressed her in dry clothing and put her on a cot to sleep. They tied a blue ribbon from around her waist to the cubicle door. This was the path that the demon driven from her body was to take.

Rebeccah Leah, Hannah, Sara, and Bryna waited anxiously

in the hall for the she-demon to appear. Faigele slept most of the afternoon, but around four o'clock only she emerged before the women. They quaked with fear as they greeted her. It was as they had suspected. Faigele was possessed by The Evil Eye. She herself was the she-demon, possibly a reincarnation of Lilith herself.

They babbled incomprehensible incantations. She lost patience. "May I leave now, you've already ruined my day. I hope you are satisfied."

"Yes," her mother said, "naturally we are satisfied." RebeccahLeah did not have the heart to tell Faigele what she and her daughters now knew. She began to weep and pray. "I'll be getting back to the slaughterhouse," said Faigele. "Father is waiting for me." From that day on, her mother and sisters wore amulets in her presence. However, when Faigele returned to the slaughterhouse and she told her father what had happened, he took off his amulet and never put it on again.

Part
THREE

1

It was a bitter cold day, several months before Judah Leib died. Abe Tarnow was busy at the men's ritualarium, and Faigele asked Hannah, her sister, to babysit. Hannah and her other sisters, Bryna and Sara, were accustomed to these requests. Two or three evenings a week, Faigele called on them.

She joined Richard at the usual time in his home, after dinner. "I have a surprise for you," he told her when she stepped inside the front hall. For several years she had not used the side entrance. Richard picked her up in his arms, spinning her around. She felt so wonderfully light and agile when he did this. "How is the fair, Faigele?" he asked, and before she could answer, he announced, "Tonight we shall read Catullus. I'm so glad I taught you Latin."

"Is reading Catullus the surprise?"

"No, my fair one." He kissed her cheeks and let his hands travel slowly down her arms. He reached for a blue and white striped hatbox sitting on the oak refectory table. The box was tied with a navy ribbon. A bunch of fresh violets in a slender sealed vial rested at the center of a big, navy bow. "Well, aren't you going to open your gift?"

He presented her with the violets before he helped her untie the ribbon. She smelled the flowers while she watched him. "Are you ready," he asked.

"Of course, I'm ready." Yet, when he held out this particular wig for her, she realized she was not prepared. Of all the wigs she had worn in his company, this one was by far the most beautiful. "Created by the master of *shietels*, Pierre Leibowitz of Boro Park," Richard said, "just for you."

"Oh, Richard, it's magnificent."

"Put it on," he urged. "The *shietel* is only part of your surprise." At that moment, a stranger entered from the other end of the hall, near the kitchen. Dressed in a pale blue barber's uniform, he had a soft, bushy moustache which reminded Faigele of her brother, Baruch's.

"Let me introduce Pierre Leibowitz. He brought this *shietel* especially for you all the way from New York. You deserve the best, my Faigele. Pierre will arrange your *shietel*. He styles *shietels* for the most fashionable Jewish orthodox women throughout the world."

Faigele followed Richard and Pierre Leibowitz into Richard's dining room. She saw that the Georgian rosewood sideboard had been miraculously converted into a long narrow dressing table on which sat a silver tray with brushes, combs, hair pins, setting lotions, and lacquers. A familiar Lemieux painting had been replaced by a fine, clear, rectangular mirror. The hairdresser pulled out a chair for her.

"What style would you like?" he asked. "This hair is better than one's own," he remarked. "I can do anything with it."

"One's own," repeated Faigele. "Yes, it is like my own," she agreed. "Certainly it's long enough," she looked closely in the mirrors. "Please don't laugh . . . I would like braids."

"Any style you wish, Madame," he acknowledged, dampening the hairs where he would work first.

Half an hour later, Faigele admired his handiwork. She asked Pierre if he would coil her braids behind her ears. Pierre proceeded to do precisely what she wanted. He tied a blue satin ribbon around each coil while Faigele kept her eyes riveted on her reflection. "You've done a superb job," she thanked Pierre. Richard shook the hairdresser's hand and Gregoire ushered him out of the dining room.

After they left, Richard stood behind Faigele, looking at their double reflection in the mirror. He placed his hands on her braided coils. He did not have to say what he was thinking.

"I'm so happy, Richard, I'm afraid."

"What are you afraid of, my Faigele?"

"I told you. Of being so content."

"Dearest Faigele," he said, "I want to take you away from Datschlav."

She didn't answer, but tears began streaming down her cheeks.

"I want you to be my wife, Faigele Berkovitch," he continued. "For almost ten years we have been having this affair. I have waited a long time. Now I want you for myself."

Ten years, she thought to herself, has it really been that long?

"Faigele, I need you. You must come away with me. Far away. I have some land in Jura, near the French-Swiss border. Recently, my old firm, Harrison, Dunlop and Bloom, offered me a job in Geneva. You've never travelled further than Boro Park, New York. Don't you want to see the world? For God's sake, Faigele, answer me."

"*Shaah!*" she scolded. "You know I can't stand when you say *Ribonu shel Olam*'s name in vain."

"I'm sorry, Faigele, but I'm upset. Do you think it's been easy for me to make this decision to leave? Don't you think I've thought about who would run the slaughterhouse? Your father is too busy and he no longer has the outside contacts. My economic situation, like yours, is tied to the community. Yet, I see no other choice for us but to leave, if we are to have a life together."

"Richard, I'm very sorry, but I cannot leave my family or my people."

He did not speak any more but began to massage her shoulders. Every inch of her body wanted him. She thought of her children and Abe Tarnow. Maybe they could get along without her. "I shall always love you," she told him. Suddenly, he pressed her wrists so firmly that he made red ridges in them. "You're hurting me, Richard."

"Faigele, you have got to marry me," he insisted. She pulled her hands away. "I didn't mean to mark you," he apologized.

"Even if you were to convert to Judaism," she said bravely,

149

"I could not marry you. I belong to Datschlav. For you, the community is different. It's just a business." Once again she looked at the red marks Richard had made on her hands and his obdurate power became known to her. "I will not leave," she said firmly.

"It's torture, what they're doing to us, Faigele. Can't you see that?"

"Richard, you know that is not true. We both have respected positions in the community. People leave us alone. What do you want of me?"

"I want you for myself. I will give you exactly six months to change your mind. For six months we will not see each other alone. Of course, you can still come by to borrow books. Gregoire will let you into the house whenever you want and you'll have your father's library for your enjoyment as always."

"You're very generous," she paused. "The wigs, will you also keep them?"

"No, there's no reason to. If you decide to come away with me, you won't be needing them, will you?"

She placed her hands on her braided coils. "I should have shunned such pleasure," she said. "But I couldn't. Everything was so lovely. Even now, this *shietel* . . ."

She made her way to the front hall where she had left her purse. The blue and white hatbox with its navy ribbon sat on the hall table. Slowly she uncoiled her braids feeling them loose and long beside her ears before she removed the wig. Then, she took her headscarf out of her handbag.

2

After Judah Leib's funeral, the Berkovitch daughters, Faigele, Sara, Bryna, and Hannah, and their husbands, Abe Tarnow, Leibel, Shmuel, and Peretz, returned to Rebeccah Leah's home to begin the official period of mourning. The living room had been cleared of furniture which was replaced by long narrow tables covered with white cloths and then fleshed over with the usual clear plastic. Bridge chairs were lined up next to each other on either side of the tables to ensure that every visitor could be seated for a glass of tea and a piece of cake or even a full meal.

Rebeccah Leah, Faigele, and Baruch were not seated at these tables but on a hard wooden bench at the entrance of the living room. According to custom, the family's black clothing was torn in several places. Baruch didn't mind the ripped, black shirt he'd been given to wear. His mood was that sombre.

First to arrive was Mendel Yehudah and his official entourage. The rebbe always travelled with a group of loyal followers should the moment arise when he felt inspired to offer thanks or supplication to *The Holy One Blessed Be He*. Keeping her distance, the rebbetzin entered next. She wheeled two dollies filled with food to assist Rebeccah Leah in feeding the mourners. Faigele's sisters unloaded platters filled with hard boiled eggs, cut-up vegetables, and fruit, four cases of bottled, pickled herring, and two dozen loaves of dark rye bread.

"Frima and the girls are bringing the rest, the meat, cakes, and drinks," reported Rebbetzin. "The desserts are all *parve*," she hastened to add.

"Think you'll have enough food," Baruch said.

"In Datschlav," Rebbetzin answered sternly, "we always have enough to eat, thank *Ribonu shel Olam*."

"Thank *Ribonu shel Olam*," the women echoed the rebbetzin on their way to the kitchen with the food. Faigele seated at the front door with her mother did not participate in their chorus.

Rebbetzin took a place on the bench between Rebeccah Leah and Faigele, while Rebbe and his entourage settled themselves in the living room. "My Judah Leib, what will become of him?" Rebeccah Leah wailed.

"At the end of the period of mourning, *The World To Come* will open for Judah Leib. He was a good man," said the rebbetzin. The authority in her voice cued the girls in the kitchen. "He was a good man," they sang obediently.

Rebbetzin began the solemn ritual comforting for a woman in mourning. It was her duty to preside over specific prayers during *shiva* visitations. She began: " 'A woman of valour who can find? For her price is far above rubies. The heart of her husband trusteth in her: and he shall have no lack of gain. She doeth him good and not evil, all the days of his life . . . ' "

"But, what shall I do?" interjected a terrified Rebeccah Leah. Tears poured down the sides of her face. "Now that he is gone, my Judah Leib, *olav-ha-shalom*, whom shall I serve? He was my love, my life. Without him I am nothing!"

"Nothing!" wailed the chorus.

"Please Rebeccah Leah, do not fear. You will be comforted." Then Rebbetzin continued: " 'She stretcheth out her hand to the poor; yea, she putteth forth her hands to the needy.' "

"The children," cried Rebeccah Leah, unable to control herself.

"We are here, Mama, we are here," cried Hannah, and soon the others came running from the kitchen.

Rebeccah Leah stood, her eyes scrubbed red with grief. Faigele joined her sisters forming a protective circle around their mother. The widow held her head in her hands while her four daughters chanted along with Rebbetzin: " 'Strength and majesty are her clothing; and she laugheth at the time to come. She openeth her mouth in wisdom; the law of loving kindness is on her tongue. She looketh to the ways of her household and eateth not the bread of idleness. Her children rise and call her happy ... ' "

"Thank *Ribonu shel Olam*, dear, dear, children," Rebeccah Leah cried as she moved back into her daughters' circle. They held on to each others' shoulders, swaying to the prescribed verse from the Book of Ruth, sung to their own Datschlaver tune: " 'The Lord, God of Israel, under whose wings thou art come to trust.' "

Rebbetzin intoned the final blessing while Rebeccah Leah and her daughters bowed in reverence to *The Holy One Blessed Be He*: " 'Open unto him the gates of righteousness and light, the gates of pity and grace. O shelter him for evermore under the cover of thy wings; and let his soul be bound up in the bond of eternal life. The Lord is his inheritance; may he rest in peace. And let us say, Amen.' "

"Amen," chanted the girls.

In the living room after prayers were offered for Judah Leib's safe journey to *The World To Come*, Mendel Yehudah addressed his followers in a gravelly voice: "There is no doubt that in the seventeen years since the creation of Datschlav, the slaughterer, Judah Leib, *olav-ha-shalom*, and his only daughter, Faigele, have led exemplary lives. Lives set apart from their fellow Datschlavers," he paused briefly, "yet, for the sake of our prosperity and well-being. Judah Leib along with Richard Vincennes and our dear Faigele have enabled this community to gain financial independence. Judah Leib had a dream and he realized it. He made the Datschlavers rich."

"You see, Mama," Faigele said, attempting to ease her anxiety. "Papa died for Datschlav. He worked hard for his people, so hard," she repeated, "and when he could no longer work, Papa gave himself to *Ribonu shel Olam!*"

Rebeccah Leah, who had been silent since Rebbetzin's final prayer, began to wail anew. Baruch attempted to console her but failed miserably. There was little comfort for her in the rebbe's eulogy. In her heart she was too afraid that her partner in life would not be her partner in death. She instinctively sensed that Judah Leib's journey to *The World To Come* would not be realized.

Not until everyone finished eating the post funeral meal did the widow begin composing herself. She sipped slowly from a glass of tea held by Faigele to her parched lips. Sighing deeply, she blew her nose into a black, lace handkerchief. But suddenly she let out a short, deep scream. It was him, The Evil One, coming to pay his respects. She veered back in terror for she longed to spit at his feet.

Despite the widow's protest, Richard Vincennes grasped her shoulders, staring into her swollen eyes. She shuddered while he offered his condolences. Turning to Faigele, he grudgingly expressed his sympathy again. Neither Rebeccah Leah or Faigele responded. However, Faigele did manage to desperately squeeze her brother's hand. "Baruch," she said nervously, "you remember Richard Vincennes ... "

"Of course," he nodded shyly.

"I'm sorry you have returned to such unfortunate news," Richard said coolly.

"My father's death has come as a terrible shock to me."

"Indeed, his death has shocked all of us," said Richard.

Rebeccah Leah sat rigidly, her posture suggesting judgment of Richard who stood so arrogantly before her. Fresh tears streamed down her crimson cheeks until her black lace handkerchief appeared soaked through.

Baruch got up from his seat to shake Richard's hand. "I believe, Mr. Vincennes," he said, "we have business to discuss."

Rebeccah Leah continued wailing, even louder than previously.

"We can talk in Judah Leib's study," Richard suggested.

Baruch nodded to his mother as he walked off with Richard, but she was too caught up in her grief to notice. Faigele anxiously folded and unfolded her hands on her lap. The two men made their way through the living room where the Rebbe and his followers were occupied, eating their noon meal.

"Your father's study," said Richard, pointing to the brass plate on the door, 'Private' written in English and Yiddish. Baruch immediately observed the incongruous opulence of his father's sanctuary, two rooms, separated by free-standing partitions, covered with grey and beige striped velvet. The second was an office with a desk and bookcases filled with more books than Baruch had seen earlier in the rebbe's study. In the first room, a reception area was tastefully furnished with a brown suede sofa and two matching cane-backed chairs flanking a finely grained rosewood coffee table. On it rested a humidor, an oversized crystal ashtray, and a green leather bound volume of Solomon Grayzel's *History of the Jews*. Both rooms were panelled in honey oak and generously carpeted with thick, grey, wall-to-wall carpet.

"Surprised?" said Richard.

"Of course, I'm surprised. How did my father get away with this?"

"Your father," replied Richard, "is not the only person who enjoyed these rooms. Your sister, Faigele, also spent many happy hours here," he paused. "You see, my friend, your father never left Datschlav but he did have some of the real world here. And privacy ... yes, he craved privacy. Faigele, too. She still does," he made certain to add.

"I always thought Faigele, like myself, wished to live a larger life than the one permitted in Datschlav but I had no idea our father shared these desires. Except when it came to business. Business fascinated him."

"Yes, I was surprised myself," said Richard dryly, "when your father made his worldly interests known to me. He had never even been to the Jewish Public Library. I took him there. After one visit, he began reading voraciously. But your sister, Faigele, she has an even greater passion for books."

"She is a remarkable woman," Baruch said. "The rebbe

always favoured her, especially after I disappointed him."

"I also find your sister exceptional," Richard paused. "Here, try one of your father's cigars. Upmanns. Your father was a man of discriminating taste. Still, he always felt guilty, 'I'll pay for all this one day,' he used to tell me."

Baruch enjoyed an expensive cigar but when he lit the Upmann he felt a wave of nausea, the same queasy feeling he had felt as a boy when his father took him proudly by the hand and they visited the Montreal abbatoirs supervised by Judah Leib.

"Your father helped make Datschlav what it is today," Richard continued. "I realize the Datschlavers are successful. Still, I find their way of life both a misery and a mystery. I have never understood it.

"Let me show you something," Richard said as he got up from the sofa. He walked across the room to the middle of the wall facing the adjoining office. He pressed in two or three places of the honeyed oak. The wall began to move. "So you think Datschlav a mystery. You say, you've never understood . . ."

The third room that Richard revealed to Baruch was a library, three of the four walls lined with books from ceiling to floor. Again, thick carpet, a burnt orange colour, and the room as tastefully furnished as the others but more tradition-al, Adam-style chairs and settees, covered in muted shade of orange, brown, and yellow. On the wall free of books, a well stocked bar including several bottles of Remy Martin, an extensive variety of wine and whiskies, including malt, Glen-livet. Six original oils hung on the wall to the right of the bar. They were Baruch's, some of his earliest paintings, the largest, *Snow in Datschlav*. A light above this one, Richard switched it on. "A fine piece of work," he complemented, acknow-ledging Baruch's name in the corner.

"It's hard to believe I once had such a heavy hand. Yet the subject matter is close to my heart. I'm obsessed. Like all good Datschlavers." Baruch stared at the painting. It drew him into its landscape. A portrait of the rebbe that glowed in the room. He was much younger Baruch remembered when he had painted it, but to Baruch, the rebbe had never looked young. The snow swirled about him, dressed in black, in contrast to the white splashing the canvas.

"This painting is still the way I see him, dominating everything in his path. You know, I cannot believe my father managed to keep a sanctuary like this in Datschlav."

Richard walked over to Judah Leib's bar. "A drink, Baruch?" he offered.

"Thanks," he said weakly.

"How about your father's favourite, Glenlivet?"

"That's fine. I'll have it straight," he said, still in a state of total bewilderment. Everything he saw, everything Richard said, overwhelmed him.

"Something to eat?" said Richard. "Your father always liked a good nibble." Richard opened the refrigerator next to the bar. Its shelves were stocked with packages of cheese, jars of pickles and olives, tins of sardines and bottles of pickled herring. Richard opened a nearby cupboard. He took out a bag of cashews, spilled the nuts into a bowl, offering some to Baruch.

"Really, no thanks. Just the drink," he managed to answer as he took a long sip of his malt whiskey. He was ready now to ask what had been on his mind since the beginning of their conversation and the unexpected tour of his father's secret world. "Please tell me about my sister."

"Baruch, what I am about to tell you will shock you more than anything you have heard or seen since your return to Datschlav. You see, when your sister became my secretary, the rebbe wanted me to befriend her, I couldn't believe it myself."

"What are you saying?" Baruch asked incredulously.

"I am saying that I have had a love affair with your sister."

"No," said Baruch, "I find that absolutely impossible to comprehend. My sister, Faigele, is a married woman. She has children." Baruch downed his drink, asking for another.

Richard took a second drink for himself too. "It appears anything is possible in Datschlav," Baruch said uncomfortably.

"I want you to know, Baruch, that your sister and I have been seeing each other for almost ten years. Everyone in the community knows about the affair." He stopped himself for a moment. "The rebbe, himself, sanctions it."

"No," objected Baruch. I do not believe you."

"Nevertheless," Richard said, "it is true." His tone changed as he explained. "When I came to this community I had my own loyalties and responsibilities. My parents had hoped that when I returned to Claremont-Ste Justine I would settle down, marry, and have children, carry on the family name. I dated women from the twin villages and from Montreal. I had many of them visit me in Datschlav until I began to fall in love with your sister. I have loved her for ten years and now I want to take her away from this place. I asked her several months ago to be my wife, but she refused." He looked away from Baruch, not wanting to speak of his rejection.

"If she were to leave with you, Datschlav would fall apart. From what I have learned since my return, Faigele, my father, and you together have managed to control the commercial life of the community. With my father gone, you, especially, can't abandon the Datschlavers. You've been working for them since 1963."

"Certainly I do not wish to abandon them," he said. "I actually thought you might consider moving back. You and Fiona Shields. The two of you could take our place. You could even have my home. A magnificent and comfortable dwelling. Your sister has spent many of her happiest hours there."

"Why hasn't she told me any of this?" Baruch asked.

"She's extremely upset. First, your father's unexpected death and now, your turning up, after all these years."

"Yes, she does have a lot on her mind. Perhaps she will confide in me soon. We haven't had much opportunity to be alone. But, in the meantime, Richard, let me make my feelings known to you, since you have spoken so freely of yours to me.

"As you probably know, my father under his will appointed me trustee to replace him in the event of his death. This has caused Rebbe Mendel Yehudah considerable distress. But I plan to tell him what I am telling you now: I cannot live in this community. I never could. I have decided to appoint my sister, Faigele, trustee in my place."

"I guessed you might do this," Richard smirked. "Don't think your sacrifice is an enticement for me," he laughed maliciously. "I have learned, my friend, that money in a place like Datschlav is worthless."

"Excuse me, Richard, my father understood far more than I ever gave him credit for. He turned out to be a very different man from the Datschlaver I once knew. But if you want to know, what I really think about this secularism of his . . . I'll tell you plainly, I think it killed him."

"Do you?" Richard said, his eyes flashing with a cold and brittle gleam.

3

Richard and Faigele had not been alone together until the day of Judah Leib's death. Richard could no longer tolerate the separation. He was in his office while Faigele was working on the books in the adjoining room. The usual noises from the kill floor, which never bothered him before, grated on his nerves. Every time an animal fell back from the stocks, he felt personally shaken.

He went next door to see Faigele, determined to find out her intentions. When he declared his feelings for her, she told him she did not wish to be disturbed. She even refused to look up from her accounting books.

"Faigele, how can you be so cold? You know you love me. We must leave this godforsaken town, you and I. We must start a new life together."

"Don't say God's name in vain," she predictably scolded.

"Is that all you have to say to me?" said Richard.

"Yes," she said dryly. "I made my decision six months ago. I will not leave my family or my people."

"Surely you have changed your mind," he stood behind her, pressing his palms into her shoulders. "Please, Faigele, come away with me. This is the last time I will ask you."

She turned in her chair to face him, giving her answer by merely shaking her head. Then, she walked out of her office and went into his, stationing herself by the kill floor window.

Richard followed. "Your decision is final?" he asked.

"Final," she said, with her back to him.

"If that's what you want," he replied angrily, stomping out of his office, slamming the door behind him. Ten years he had given to this woman. Tried to show her the ways of the world. "The ungrateful bitch," he muttered under his breath.

Faigele watched from the window as Richard entered the killing emporium. The routine of the slaughter provided her with an unexpected feeling of tranquility, even though the pace was as hectic as ever, Datschlavers in grey striped kimonas and grey aprons rushing about, their sidelocks flying, kimona coattails held in place by their apron strings.

Four senior students on exchange from Boro Park, New York, in Datschlav every Monday through Thursday, were busy sorting tongues, thymus glands, livers, lungs, and brains at the organ table. Other Datschlaver students, sitting on a nearby bench, watched the Boro Park boys trim, stamp, and hang these organs on free-standing racks next to the cutting table. As soon as they finished, they rushed to the centre of the kill floor where the next animal dropped from its hook, waiting for its chest cavity to be slit.

Her father stood close by, selecting a blonde student with a rosy complexion, button nose, and perfectly combed sidelocks, so long they hung to his shoulders, to draw the knife through the dead animal's upper torso. As soon as the young man cut, Judah Leib stuck his hand inside the slaughtered animal, giving a thorough swish. He removed his bloody arm, directing his students to follow his example.

She saw Richard watching her father from where he was standing next to the stocks. Usually he didn't go on to the kill floor. Now, like her, he watched and waited.

Judah Leib gave the okay sign after his examination. Faigele knew this meant the animal had no adhesions on its lungs. He wiped his hands on his apron and made ready to plunge his hand a second time inside the dead animal in order to sever the lungs from the chest cavity with his sharp knife. He carried them over to the cutting table; then he returned to the stocks. On a nearby shelf, he kept the whetstones that he used for sharpening his knives. Usually he spent ten minutes of every hour sharpening and polishing his instruments, but today Richard interrupted him.

Faigele could see they were arguing. Her father, clearly agitated, waved his hands in the air while Richard stood stiffly, his hands in his pockets, a menacing stare on his face.

Faigele began to worry. She paced nervously for several minutes until she realized that the activity on the kill floor had come to an abrupt halt. There wasn't a sound from below. Fearfully, she approached the window. When she looked down she saw her father's students bent over his body. She watched as they covered his head with his slaughterer's apron before they carried him out of the abbatoir.

On the last day of *shiva* a specially convened meeting took place at the home of Mendel Yehudah. The rebbe took his usual place at the head of the table. Richard, who had called the meeting, faced the rebbe at the opposite end. The rebbetzin, seated next to her husband, glanced uncomfortably at Richard. Across from her sat Abe Tarnow and Fiona Shields. Baruch was seated on Richard's right, while Faigele, on his left, faced her brother. All the assembled listened intently to Richard, who insisted on re-living the final moments of their beloved ritual slaughterer.

"It is hard to believe, that only a few days ago, Judah Leib was still among us . . . " Richard began. The listeners shuffled uncomfortably in their seats. "I was planning to ask permission to marry Faigele," he told everyone. "A man is determined when he thinks he's in love. For ten years I have had Faigele as my mistress. Everyone in Datschlav knows. Even her husband, Abe Tarnow. Even the rebbe, himself." As Richard spoke, no one looked at him, except Faigele, whose piercing gaze seemed to penetrate his very being. But he was oblivious to her staring and the others' obvious embarrassment. His monologue was a serious confession and he was determined to proceed.

"For six months we stopped seeing each other privately, until a few days ago, when I couldn't stand the separation any longer. I was in my office at the slaughterhouse. Faigele was working on the books in her adjoining office. We abided by our decision and didn't show each other any affection. But I was tormented. I knew I had to speak to her, to persuade her to be my wife.

"I went next door, determined to have my way. When I told her I loved her, she asked me not to disturb her. I couldn't believe how cold she was. Yet I persisted, begging her to come away with me, to leave Datschlav." Richard stopped a moment to look at Faigele. But now she refused to look at her former lover. Baruch sat with his head buried in his hands, totally bewildered and devastated, while Richard continued, unburdening himself. "I was attracted to Faigele when I first met her in the Datschlaver synagogue on Jeanne Mance in Montreal. She had hair then," he added, "beautiful, black hair."

Rebbe Mendel Yehudah pulled his prayershawl over his head so that only his face peeked through. He rocked back and forth, his lips moving silently. When the telephone rang, he didn't answer it. The rebbetzin picked up the receiver. "No calls," she told Lifsky, "except emergencies."

The rebbe prayed fervently, tuning out Richard as much as he could.

Yet Richard went on. "Faigele refused to come away with me. She told me she wished to remain with her family and her people. I was disappointed and angry. I stomped out of her office, slamming the door behind me, feeling capable of anything as I made my way downstairs to the kill floor. Ten years I had given to Faigele. Tried to show her the ways of the world. What for I asked myself?

"I walked over to the stocks and waited beside the shelf where Judah Leib kept his whetstones. Usually he spent ten minutes of every hour sharpening his instruments. When he had finished checking his previously slaughtered animal for lung adhesions, he came over to where I stood. I told him that I wanted to marry his daughter. I even told him that I would convert. Become a Jew. Not a Datschlaver, but a Jew, nevertheless.

"I could see he was upset. He wiped his hands on his apron and walked over to the cutting table where his students were busy with the lungs he had just severed. One end of a hose had been fastened to an air pump, the other to the severed organ. Judah Leib pressed a button on the side of the cutting table and waited for the lungs to expand." Richard paused, "You're all familiar with the pattern of the kill?" Then, he turned deliberately to Faigele's brother, "You do remember, don't you, Baruch?"

Baruch looked up, his face pale and drawn.

Painstakingly, Richard explained. "You'll be interested to know how efficient your father and his team of slaughterers became. The average kill per day was one thousand, one hundred and ten, that's a hundred and eleven cattle slaughtered every day in each of the ten sections of the abbatoir."

Baruch showed no surprise. He was ready for the entire story. He could hear his father's voice. Perhaps he was speaking to him from *The World To Come*: "One day, Baruch, these knives will be yours."

"Judah Leib returned to the stocks where I was waiting." He began sharpening his knife on the whetstone. I decided to press him further about Faigele. " 'So what's wrong with asking my daughter, or what about the rebbe? Why are you asking me?' He stopped sharpening and began buffing his knife, rubbing his long thumb nail over the smooth, rectangular blade: 'Perfect,' he said, 'Perfect,' and then, he looked at me as coolly as his precious Faigele had looked at me a few minutes earlier. 'I'm sorry, Richard,' he said, 'I cannot help you.' "

"Once more my anger welled up inside me, and I confronted him with the truth. 'There is no money left in Datschlav,' I told him sharply. 'I've transferred all the community's savings to my bank account in Switzerland. Tomorrow, I plan to leave Datschlav.'

"Judah Leib waved his hands in protest. At first he was so upset he could not speak. He actually brandished his slaughterer's knife at me. Then, suddenly, he regained his composure. He put down his knife on the sharpening table and began to work on it anew, even though a few moments earlier he had been satisfied with its sharpness. While he worked he asked me how I managed to abscond the community's funds. Once again, I told him the truth, reminding him of the monthly transfer payments he had signed during the last six months, recalling for him how during this period he would sign every document I gave him without reading it. I knew six months ago after Faigele abandoned me that I had to look out for myself.

"Woman," Richard shouted at Faigele, "you're a foolish, loyal Datschlaver. I can see this clearly." He no longer cared what he said to her or to the others. Now, it was time to disclose the lurid detail. "Your father gave the signal for the resumption of the kill. The next animal's head was locked in the stocks. Judah Leib drew his shining, rectangular blade along the animal's throat. The animal seemed to be smiling at me," Richard laughed. "I felt tired," he admitted. "The stock opened, the animal fell back. Judah Leib turned to me and said, 'Death is painless, my friend.' Then, he went to the centre of the floor where the slitting of the animal's chest cavity takes place. I stayed back, next to the empty stock.

"He stood as usual among his students. I thought he must be giving them instructions. I liked to watch Judah Leib on the floor. He was an expert, so methodical, so definite. I envied the certainty of his craft, the art of killing. I felt more determined than ever to leave Datschlav, but I began to feel remorse for absconding the community's funds. I decided to tell Judah Leib that I would return some of the money. After seventeen years of hard work on my part, the Datschlavers' position in the French-Canadian countryside was secure. Even though I no longer approved of their way of life, I decided I didn't want the community left penniless.

"I wanted to tell your father my decision, even though I knew I couldn't talk with him until the next break. The timing on the floor is crucial and can never be interrupted unless there is an emergency. Still, I couldn't wait, so I rushed over to the middle of the room. I pushed my way in among the students. There was the animal he had just slaughtered, lying on the floor with its front slit, sternum to belly. Beside the carcass lay Judah Leib, his face to the floor. When the Datschlavers turned him over, his knife fell out of his hands. I could not believe my eyes. Judah Leib's jugular lay totally exposed; he had slit his throat as clean as the cow's. His blood and the blood of the last animal he had slaughtered before his suicide commingled as the hose on the kill floor swished, sending a red tinged river down the drain."

Richard wiped his forehead. He was perspiring profusely. Still, he was not quite finished. "The immediate family and the good people of Datschlav were told that Judah Leib had had an accident. But everyone on the floor and everyone here, now, knows the truth.

"Of course," Richard said, "*The Chevra Kadisha*, the holy assembly who mended Judah Leib's broken neck before wrapping him in his shroud, also knew the truth."

Finally Richard addressed Baruch concerning financial matters. "As for your trusteeship, my friend, it seems there is no money for you to be trustee of. Datschlav, I assure you, is quite bankrupt, and I personally have had a change of heart. I shall stick by my decision as Faigele, your sister, has stuck by hers. I shall not give a penny of the Datschlav trust money back to this ridiculous community."

Faigele rose from the conference table. Her white skin contrasted sharply with her black dress of mourning. Her lips were parched and she passed her tongue over them as she spoke. "I have never been a true Datschlaver. I hereby proclaim myself no longer a member of this community. Tomorrow I will return to Montreal. Datschlav is a dream," she pronounced venomously. "Richard Vincennes knows it. I know it. My brother, Baruch, and Fiona Shields know it, and my dear father, Judah Leib, *olav-ha-shalom*, knew it too, before he took his own life."

Abe Tarnow wept into the sleeve of his black gaberdine. Rebbe Mendel Yehudah Kasarkofski raised his head from the table. In shame, he had laid his head there, covering it totally with his prayershawl. Now, he stood slowly, turning towards the east. Swaying back and forth he prayed quietly, without his quorum.